17868

RETURN
to
HARMONY

$\mathcal{R}$ETURN *to* $\mathcal{H}$ARMONY

A NOVEL BY
JANETTE OKE
&
T. DAVIS BUNN

BETHANY HOUSE PUBLISHERS
MINNEAPOLIS, MINNESOTA 55438

17868 F
OKE

Return to Harmony
Copyright © 1996
Janette Oke & T. Davis Bunn

Cover by Dan Thornberg,
Bethany House Publishers staff artist.

Published by Bethany House Publishers
A Ministry of Bethany Fellowship, Inc.
11300 Hampshire Avenue South
Minneapolis, Minnesota 55438

Printed in the United States of America.

Library of Congress Cataloging-in-Publication Data

CIP applied for

ISBN 1-55661-878-6   CIP

FOR JEAN

*With thankfulness to God
for the many shared dreams,
laughter, tears, and treasures.
All that a sister was meant to be—
mentor, supporter, encourager,
and special friend.*

JANETTE OKE, known and loved for her godly strength, warmth, and delightful writing style, is a nationally acclaimed author. The recipient of the coveted Gold Medallion Award for fiction, she was also presented with the 1992 President's Award from the Evangelical Christian Publishers Association for her significant contribution to Christian fiction.

T. DAVIS BUNN is an award-winning writer and extraordinarily creative wordsmith who has published over fifteen novels with Bethany House Publishers. From fiction of high drama and intrigue to very quiet, heartwarming stories that explore the intricacies of human relationships and the constancy of divine love, he has enriched the lives of readers of all ages and interests.

As part of the Bethany House Publishers family of authors, Janette and Davis met at booksellers' conventions and became friends. Out of these occasional meetings and continuing correspondence has grown a mutual appreciation for each other's calling and strengths as Christian novelists. Eventually came the idea of combining those strengths in a collaborative effort that has resulted in the writing of *Return to Harmony*.

Janette says, "Because our writing styles are quite different, we weren't sure at first if or how this was going to work. But as we began those first discussions and plans, we were surprised and pleased with the way the story idea began coming together and growing into characters and a plot we both felt good about." Davis adds, "I am deeply gratified and honored that Janette was willing to attempt this writing partnership."

From the beginning of their team effort, both authors felt that the resulting novel would be something "in between" what they each would do on their own. Beyond the unique collaboration, their hope is that their readers will be as captivated by the characters and story as they were in the development.

Janette's well-loved "signature," the emotional connections to her readers through ordinary details of her characters' lives, is showcased in this new setting as Davis brings his descriptive talents, touches of humor, and plot intricacies to this innovative writing venture.

Books by Janette Oke

Janette Oke's Reflections on the Christmas Story
The Red Geranium
Return to Harmony (with T. Davis Bunn)
Nana's Gift

SEASONS OF THE HEART

Once Upon a Summer   Winter Is Not Forever
The Winds of Autumn   Spring's Gentle Promise

LOVE COMES SOFTLY

Love Comes Softly   Love's Unending Legacy
Love's Enduring Promise   Love's Unfolding Dream
Love's Long Journey   Love Takes Wing
Love's Abiding Joy   Love Finds a Home

CANADIAN WEST

When Calls the Heart   When Breaks the Dawn
When Comes the Spring   When Hope Springs New

WOMEN OF THE WEST

The Calling of Emily Evans   A Bride for Donnigan
Julia's Last Hope   Heart of the Wilderness
Roses for Mama   Too Long a Stranger
A Woman Named Damaris   The Bluebird and the Sparrow
They Called Her Mrs. Doc   A Gown of Spanish Lace
The Measure of a Heart   Drums of Change

DEVOTIONALS

The Father Who Calls   Father of My Heart
The Father of Love   Faithful Father

Janette Oke: A Heart for the Prairie
Biography of Janette Oke by Laurel Oke Logan

The Oke Family Cookbook
by Barbara Oke and Deborah Oke

9605

Books by T. Davis Bunn

The Quilt
The Gift
The Messenger
The Music Box

The Maestro
The Presence
Promises to Keep
Return to Harmony (with Janette Oke)
Riders of the Pale Horse

The Priceless Collection

Secret Treasures of Eastern Europe

1. *Florian's Gate*
2. *The Amber Room*
3. *Winter Palace*

Rendezvous With Destiny

1. *Rhineland Inheritance*
2. *Gibraltar Passage*
3. *Sahara Crosswind*
4. *Berlin Encounter*
5. *Istanbul Express*

CHAPTER ONE

JODIE RACED DOWN the dusty street, her calico skirt gathered in one hand, the other trailing a piece of colored bunting. The broad ribbon streaming out behind her was a remnant of the parade marking President Woodrow Wilson's reelection campaign. Her leather lace-up shoes still felt clumsy and awkward after almost a month of discomfort. She had received them for her thirteenth birthday, and it was a present which still rankled. Her mother had declared it was time for a proper young lady to have proper shoes, to quit all this running around barefoot, that she had given in to Jodie's pleadings quite long enough. Good ankle-high lace-ups tied nice and firm were the answer, and it had not mattered how much Jodie complained. And she had complained quite a bit.

Jodie slowed her skipping at the sight of a vaguely familiar form. The smaller girl crouched on the bottom step of a porch, head bowed down on her knees, her shoulders bent and shaking.

The streamer settled unheeded into the dust of the sidewalk as Jodie approached the small figure. "What's the matter?"

The young girl was sobbing so hard it took her a few

minutes to get the words out. "I . . . found me a . . . a puppy," she finally managed between hiccoughs.

Jodie hesitated a moment. Bethan Keane was as much a stranger as anyone near her own age could be in the town of Harmony. She was a quiet, shy little thing with a riot of copper curls around a small, pale face. She scarcely had the nerve to say she was there when the teacher called out her name. She was an easy target for teasing from the other kids, because she was so small and so quiet, and because of her eye. Bethan had a lazy eye, was what Jodie's father had explained. Her father, who ran the town apothecary, knew all about things like that. How could an eye be lazy? Jodie wanted to know. But her father did not answer. He seldom had time for most of Jodie's questions. Jodie had heard him tell a customer that if he answered even half of Jodie's questions he would not have time for anything else. Now, as Jodie stood and looked down at Bethan's sniffling little form, she saw how the left eye swam out to one side, just as though it really was lazy.

Jodie squatted down on the stoop beside Bethan. "Why does finding a puppy make you cry? Most kids would be—" she searched for the appropriate word, groping for one she had just heard her mother use, "egstatic."

That opened the faucets up wide. "My momma won't let me keep it. Not even for one night."

So it was settled indeed, then. Bethan's momma, Moira Keane, was known as a woman of her word. Jodie's mother said that Moira's severe exterior hid a heart of solid gold. Maybe so, her father had replied, but that exterior was about as yielding as the pit of a Georgia peach.

Jodie inspected the puppy, reaching out to touch the sides that shivered with excitement, or nervousness, and declared, "Sure is a scrawny little runt."

"He's hungry. I fed him some milk and meat scraps and a piece of bread, and he's still hungry."

One small hand stroked the puppy's back. The bones of its spine jutted up through the soft fur, and every rib was clearly visible. "I think maybe he was 'bandoned."

"Abandoned," Jodie corrected, and examined the puppy with the experienced eye of a country girl with the added benefit of a father knowledgeable about medicine. The trembling little beast was a mongrel, probably part hound and certainly the runt of the litter. But the eyes were clear, and the dog looked intelligent and eager despite being so weak from hunger. "Can't be more than a few months old," she observed.

Bethan nodded and sniffed and wiped her eyes. Jodie noted that a pink ribbon from one of the girl's braids was tied around the puppy's neck. Every once in a while the puppy would sit down and work at it with one paw, but then would lose interest and return to staring at Bethan with adoring eyes. "Momma says I've got to let it go. But if I do, who will feed it?" she mourned.

Jodie gazed at Bethan, whose hand kept brushing at the puppy with such love and whose chin still trembled with her sorrow. Jodie felt herself touched in a way she couldn't explain at the girl's reluctance to put the small pup back out on his own with no one to tend to his needs—abandoned once more.

A shadow fell over them. "Hey, what'cha got?" Jodie looked up to find Kirsten Sloane staring at the puppy. Kirsten's father ran the local butcher's shop, and her mother was the sternest teacher in their school. She was the tallest girl in the class, bigger even than many of the boys, and somewhat of a snob and a tyrant. She took one look that swept in Jodie, Bethan, and the small puppy all in a glance, sneered at them, then turned to call back down the street, "Come look! The runt's found herself a runt!"

Bethan's chin quivered, but she kept her voice steady as she said, "Leave my puppy alone."

Kirsten seemed to enjoy tormenting those smaller and weaker, and Bethan was often her favorite victim. Her eyes glinted as she reached for the little dog. "I can touch him if I want."

Without thinking, Jodie coiled herself up and sprang at Kirsten. The larger girl was caught completely off guard and went sprawling in the dust. For one moment Jodie felt triumph, then surprise. She had not expected her effort to bring such immediate results. But the satisfaction soon turned to concern when she glimpsed an adult shape coming their way. She put on a contrite expression and reached down to Kirsten. "I'm sorry. Here—let me help you. I . . . I stumbled."

Kirsten slapped the hand away and scrambled to her feet, fists clenched at her sides. "You did it on purpose! I'm gonna—"

"Here, here, what's this?" Miss Charles, the new teacher at their school, was upon them in an instant. "Now just a minute, Kirsten. Didn't you hear Jodie tell you it was an accident?"

Jodie stepped back and breathed a sigh of relief. For reasons she could not quite understand, Miss Charles had taken an instant liking to her. The knowledge made her feel safe enough to say, in a slightly smug tone, "I don't know what happened—I must have slipped."

"Did not," Kirsten hissed between her teeth. The look she turned on Jodie said clearly that she knew what had happened and was in no mind to let it pass without retribution, even though she felt unable to do anything about it at the moment.

"If I catch the slightest wind of anything more between you two," the teacher said, reading the situation correctly, "I will take it up personally with your mothers. Do I make myself perfectly clear?"

Kirsten subsided to an angry scowl and Jodie lowered her eyes in submission and nodded slowly.

"I asked you a question," Miss Charles said, turning to Kirsten and using her warning voice.

Kirsten gave a single nod, then turned and fled, shouting over her shoulder as she ran, "All right for *you*, Jodie Harland!"

Jodie turned back to Miss Charles and gave her a proper curtsey, something she ordinarily would have done only after pleadings from her mother. Or maybe a nickel from her dad. "Thank you, Miss Charles. I'm sorry to have disturbed your day."

"Not at all, Jodie. I do hope this is the end of it." She smiled at them both, turned her gaze on the swiftly vanishing Kirsten, then back to the two before her. "You girls have a nice afternoon, now."

When the teacher had strolled on, Bethan turned to Jodie with eyes wide in surprise. "You did that for me?"

Jodie was a little surprised herself. "I couldn't let Kirsten pick on you like that."

"Thank you," Bethan said, her voice little more than a whisper. Before Jodie could respond, she turned solemn and said, "But you fibbed to the teacher."

"Not really." Jodie thought it over, then decided, "Not a lot, anyway."

"But you did. I heard you with my own ears." There was no real condemnation in her voice. Only quiet certainty. "If we're gonna be friends, you have to promise

15

never to do that again. It's not right—it's one of the Comman'ments."

"Well, I'll be," Jodie said, using one of her father's favorite expressions. She sank down beside the smaller girl, too astonished to stand any longer. "You really mean it, don't you?"

"'Course I do," Bethan said. "That is, if you want to be my friend. Seems like we've already made a good start. Friends help each other. That's what you just did for me."

"I don't have many friends," Jodie confessed, taking up Bethan's train of thought.

"You're lucky," Bethan replied in her quiet and solemn way. "I don't have any at all. Except for Dylan. And he's my brother, so I guess he doesn't count."

Suddenly Jodie leapt to her feet. "What's the matter?" Bethan asked quickly, looking around as if expecting Kirsten to descend on them again.

Jodie was already starting down the road. "Come on—it's almost noon," she beckoned Bethan. "I've got an idea. We need to hurry, though. Momma says I have to be home in time for dinner."

Bethan rose to follow. "But where are we going?"

Jodie started to run. "The puppy needs a home, doesn't he?"

———— ✿ ————

Harmony of 1915 was a growing community, but full of traditional farming spirit. Homes were places of calm, comfort, and security. Trees were old and broad and as stately as the big central buildings around the town square. Harmony was the county seat, so the main intersection was firmly anchored by a courthouse and state building, both fashioned of gray granite. They offered a sense of grandeur and permanence to the town, dressing up the surrounding low red-brick shops in the downtown.

No one would ever think to lock their doors in Harmony. Sitting on the front porch meant folks were home to visitors. Much was made of little things—a teething baby, a new foal from a prize horse, a birthday, an anniversary. It was a way for folks to say that they cared and belonged.

It was warm for an early April day, and visitors from the countryside were already slipping into customary summer ways. Farm wagons pulled up under the great shade trees were filled with market produce covered by layers of fresh hay. Horses waited with the patience of hard workers, munching idly from feed bags and swiping at the year's first crop of flies. Farming mothers spread out bright linens and began unpacking hampers, while their kids danced with the excitement of having pennies to buy Cheerwine and root beer and maybe even a licorice whip.

Harmony stood at the center of eastern North Carolina's farm belt. It grew faster than other regional towns, both because it lay on the main road connecting Richmond to Fayetteville and on down to Columbia, and because the train from Raleigh to the Wilmington port stopped there. Harmony was also the farthest inland a barge could travel on the nearby Yancey River. Farming families from as far away as Greenville and Selma traveled in to sell their produce, have their chests thumped and wills made, and to search for the special dry-goods not carried by general stores in villages closer to home.

Jodie turned left behind the courthouse, scampered

along a narrow dusty track, and came out in front of a long row of wooden shanties. "I sure hope he's home."

Bethan walked more slowly, looking around in astonishment. "I didn't even know these were back here," she said in a breathless voice that spoke both of the hurried trip and the shivery awe that she felt at being in an unknown part of town.

"I love to explore," Jodie explained, stepping onto the third shanty's narrow front porch and knocking on the door. "Momma's always going on to me about it. She says I was born with a restless spirit."

A querulous voice called, "Who's there?"

"Me, Mr. Russel. And I brought a friend—two of them." Jodie turned to where Bethan waited a safe distance away nestling the puppy and said in a low voice, "It's okay. He used to work around the place for my daddy. But his eyesight's gone. Momma comes back every once in a while and makes sure he's all right."

"That she does, that she does. Your momma's a purebred saint, little lady." Apparently the man's hearing was just fine, for he spoke his words from somewhere within the strange little home. The screen door squeaked open to reveal a wizened old man in stained pants, suspenders, and collarless shirt. His leathery face was crowned by a mass of white hair. He squinted down at Jodie, then grinned to reveal more gaps than teeth. "Ain't many folks who'd take the time to see how an old soldier was doing."

"Mr. Russel fought in the Civil War," Jodie announced.

"Ain't nobody interested in such goings-on anymore." The man peered vaguely in Bethan's direction. "Come on up here close so I can get a look at you, little girl. I ain't gonna hurt nobody."

Bethan stirred reluctantly, but Jodie motioned her

closer and spoke again. "I heard Momma tell Daddy your dog passed on."

He turned his attention back to Jodie. "Nigh on three weeks now," he said, a tremor in his voice. "Sure did leave a big hole in my life. That little guy was wonderful company for an old feller."

He looked back toward Bethan as she took a pair of tentative steps his way. "What's your name, gal?"

"Bethan, sir." She pronouced it to rhyme with "Megan."

"Now ain't that an interesting name," he commented. "Where'd your folks come upon it?"

The old man's friendliness seemed to overcome Bethan's shyness, and she spoke quickly. "It's Welsh. Momma came from there—Wales, I mean—when she was a little girl. It's part of Britain. My real name is Elizabeth Ann, but Momma shortened it to Bethan. That was her grandmother's name. Daddy says she probably had the naming all planned from the beginning, and he wishes she'd have just gone and done it up front."

"Bethan's momma is used to getting her own way," Jodie explained, reciting something she had heard her daddy say.

Bethan stared at how the old man squinted in his effort to concentrate on distinguishing the new face. "I've got a bad eye too," Bethan said frankly. "But only when I get tired. Momma says it's lazy, and it came from Daddy's side of the family."

"Well, is that a fact? Let's hope it don't ever get no lazier," he said with good humor but a tone of concern in his voice as well. He bent over. "What's that you got there in your hands?"

"It's a little puppy," Jodie said before Bethan could answer. "Bethan found him. Her momma won't let her keep him. And he needs someone to care for him or he'll get hungry again. And he's lonely."

"That makes two of us, then, don't it?" Work-stained hands reached over. "Mind if I hold him for a minute?"

Bethan hesitated, then with a nod from Jodie handed the puppy over, her eyes watching carefully as the elderly man scooped him in his big brown hands and held him tenderly against his stained shirt. The little puppy instantly tried to reach up and lick the wizened face. The gap-tooth grin reappeared. "Well, ain't he a friendly little feller. Feels like all skin and bones, though."

"He needs a good feeding," Jodie agreed.

"And lots of love," Bethan added, her voice carrying a hint of bittersweet.

"I'll be giving this little feller a good home, if you decide to let me keep him," the elderly man said with warmth. Then he added, "And mind, you can come and see him anytime you like."

Bethan's face brightened. "That'd be the next best thing to keeping him myself, wouldn't it?"

"Sure would." The old man lifted the excited little dog higher in his arms, letting the cold nose nuzzle under his chin. "And you'd be doing me a passel of good to boot. Everybody on this earth is in need of a friend."

Jodie nodded agreement, looking in wonder at Bethan. She had never realized how true that was. Until now.

CHAPTER TWO

WHEN BETHAN SAT UP in bed it was not yet six. Already the air was heavy with smells and dust and new sun. The smells always seemed stronger to her in the morning, sharp enough to smack her awake. She slid from her high four-poster bed, crossed to the window, pushed the white curtains aside, and reveled in the new day.

Everything was bright and clean and fresh and waiting for her. Even the hog pen, which Momma often complained was too close to the house. To Bethan, it seemed perfect where it was, just as Daddy always said. She liked it when her folks talked about the hogs, which was a strange thing to say about listening to her parents argue. But Daddy always said Momma only talked about the hog pen when everything was right with the world. Momma never denied it, but instead would bustle about in the way she did when she was caught out and embarrassed about something, and say that it never paid to be content. Contentment was when trouble got ready to pounce. Complaining about the hogs was as close to perfection as Momma ever wanted to come.

Bethan leaned on the windowsill and drew in deeply

of the morning air. Turning back into her room, she filled herself with the odors of home—the fruit hanging heavy on the orchard trees, tobacco ripening in her uncle's fields, the animals, and the promise of coming activities with a best friend. Today was the last day of freedom before school started again. Bethan had spent long hours planning out this final free day with Jodie. She leaned against the windowsill and said the words silently to herself, *best friend*. Sometimes she still had trouble believing it was so.

She walked over and hopped back onto her bed. It had been her grandparents', and had a high frame topped by a thick goosedown mattress and intricately carved posts. Bethan loved the feel of the grooved wood under her fingers and the springiness. She didn't take the time now to enjoy the slight bounce but picked up the Bible from the nearby table and settled it on her lap. She had not told anyone, but she was trying to read the entire Bible, cover to cover, in one year. Reading did not come easy to her, especially now when she was struggling through Isaiah. But then she came to, "Hear, ye deaf; and look, ye blind, that ye may see." *I'm not really blind*, she mused, *but I sure would like to see better.*

Bethan did not want anyone to know about her Bible-reading goal in case she could not finish on time. So she read alone, pronouncing with slowness and difficulty some of the long, strange words, one outstretched finger leading the way across the page.

She closed the book and her eyes, praying as she did every morning for her new best friend.

"Bethan!" Her mother's voice drifted upward from the bottom of the stairs. "Come on down for breakfast, honey, your father's about ready to leave." Then with more urgency, "Dylan! If you make me come up these stairs one more time, you won't sit down for a week!"

Bethan scampered over to the door and called down quickly to keep the nearly inevitable from happening, "It's okay, Momma, I can hear him—I think he's up."

"Then your ears are better than mine, child. You'd best be right."

Bethan waited for her mother to return to the kitchen, then hurried to the end of the hall and entered her brother's room. But it was not movement which she had heard, only the sound of Dylan snoring. Bethan quietly shut the door behind her and moved over to the bed. Dylan could sleep twelve hours and wake up tired. Their daddy often proclaimed that his son could sleep through the Second Coming and not even roll over. Momma always snorted at that and replied that her husband chose the strangest reasons to take pride in his family.

"You've made me fib to Momma," Bethan exclaimed in dismay. "I thought you were already up."

Bethan did what she often had to, which was pull the pillow out from beneath Dylan's head, then bounce his shoulder up and down with both hands. If she didn't have him up soon, their momma would be up the stairs for sure and they'd both be in trouble. "Breakfast is on the table," she whispered hoarsely in his exposed ear.

"Five minutes," came the mumbled reply.

Bethan shook harder, hearing the measured tread begin the climb. "I can hear Momma on the stairs," she said anxiously.

With a speed that belied his inert position of the moment before, Dylan exploded from the covers. He reached blindly for the trousers hanging from the back of his chair, pulled them up and tucked his nightshirt's long edge in as far as he could, snapped on the suspenders, and scrambled to the door.

Moira's foot hit the fourth step, and in her final-warning voice she called, "All right, Dylan—"

"I'm up, Momma, I'm up," he called back breathlessly.

The footsteps stopped, paused for a moment, then retreated. "Tell your sister to hurry up, too."

"Yes, ma'am." Dylan allowed himself to lean against the wall as he dragged the hair out of his face. "That was too close for comfort," he breathed in a conspiratorial whisper.

"She's gonna catch you one of these days," warned Bethan.

"Not so long as I've got me a guardian angel living just down the hall." Sleepily he searched the front of his trousers. "What's the matter with these pants?"

"You might try putting them on the other way around," Bethan said with a giggle, then turned to hasten back down the hall to dress.

In a matter of minutes Bethan appeared in the kitchen looking reasonably calm and decently attired.

"Well, finally. What took you so long, child?" her mother asked. Moira Keane, Welsh, was the practical one of the family. Her parents had brought her to America when she was still a child, but Moira had never completely lost the lilting accent of her first homeland.

Before Bethan could venture a reply, the woman hurried on, "Never mind. Come let me look at your eye."

Bethan gave a silent sigh as she stood before her mother for the daily inspection. This was the hardest moment of every day. Moira turned from the stove, bent over, and looked hard at her left eye. The lazy one, so the doctor said. Though how anything could be lazy when everyone made her work it so hard was beyond Bethan.

"Looks all right," Moira said, holding up one finger. "Close the other eye."

Bethan cupped her right eye, and with her left eye began following her mother's finger as it moved purposefully back and forth before her face. Dylan chose that moment to step quietly into the kitchen. He raised a finger behind his mother's back and started waving it all around the room. Bethan could not help but giggle. Without looking up, Moira said crossly, "That's about enough out of you, young man. You already are skating on thin ice this morning."

As Dylan slid into his seat, Moira finished her morning ritual and reached forward to kiss her daughter's forehead. "It looks fine this morning. No patch for you today."

"Thank you, Momma," Bethan replied in quiet relief. The eyepatch was the bane of Bethan's existence. She had to wear it every evening, when the left eye had the greatest tendency to wander. By covering the right eye Bethan was forced to consciously bring the left one into focus. But every couple of weeks or so the eye wandered even when she woke up, and then she had to wear the patch all day long. Much to her relief, it had not yet happened on a school morning.

"The last day before school starts," her father said, leaning over and accepting Bethan's peck with a smile. "Going to spend it with Jodie?"

"Chalk and cheese, that pair," her mother said, setting a steaming plate of oatmeal down in front of Dylan. "Different in every way. Never seen the like in all my born days."

"Well, now," Gavin said, which was about as close as he ever came to arguing with his wife. And strangely enough, those two words, even when mildly spoken, were enough to subdue Moira's somewhat contentious ways. "It only seems so, the way I see things. Down deep, that pair are similar as two peas in the same pod. Not so different, when you take a closer look."

Moira said no more.

"Thank you, Momma," Bethan said when the plate was set down in front of her. She did not know exactly what her father meant by his statement that she and Jodie were alike, but she hoped with all her heart that what he said was so.

Moira settled her own plate on the table and took her chair. Gavin bowed his head with the others and prayed, "For all your many blessings, Father, most especially this family, do I give thanks. Guide us and bless us all this day, and bless this food to our bodies."

"Keep us on your path, and bring us all home safely at day's end," her mother closed, as she always did. "In Jesus' precious name, amen."

Her father opened his eyes, surveyed the plate before him, and said what he always did before every meal, "This looks fit for a king, Momma."

Bethan's gray eyes opened, met and returned her father's smiling gaze. Gavin Keane was, as far as his daughter was concerned, the most wonderful father on earth. His love of life spilled over everything like a full stream. When Bethan was alone, she liked to repeat to herself the favorite descriptions she had heard neighbors say of him. Words like a jolly soul, an easygoing fellow, and a truly contented man. She loved it when people praised him, loved how even her no-nonsense mother would reply with a gleam of pride. His work for the state farm board was respected. Farmers liked him because he was a farmer himself, one of their own who treated them fairly. Bethan loved him because he made her feel special, cared-for, secure in the home he had provided.

Bethan loved their mostly country home on the edge of town. It stood at the border of the old Keane family homestead. Bethan's uncle, her daddy's older brother, lived in the old farmhouse and worked the larger fields. Her own family kept a few pigs and cows, had a prize brood of Leghorns and Rhode Island Reds, a vegetable garden, and a three-acre fruit orchard. Bethan doubted that her daddy could ever be content without a little bit of farming to begin and end each day. She couldn't imagine him without a cow to milk or a litter of pigs to call to the feeding trough.

Gavin looked fondly across the big country table at his daughter and asked, "Ready for school tomorrow, daughter?"

"I'll never be ready," Bethan declared, and felt a cloud slip over her day.

"Your little friend is ready," her mother stated. "I asked her the same thing yesterday, and she told me she had already started reading some of her books."

"Jodie is a lot smarter than me," Bethan said, not minding the truth because it was her best friend she described. "All the teachers say it. I heard Miss Charles say Jodie was the most remarkish student she'd ever taught."

"Remarkable, child, remarkable," Moira corrected, then turned to her husband and said, "I wish a little of that smartness would rub off, I surely do."

"Don't you worry about Bethan," Dylan declared, pushing his empty plate away. Dylan was four years older, sturdy and pleasant. He possessed the best of both his parents, a strong sense of duty and a jolly eye for the ridiculous. Some felt he was far too handsome for his own good, but he never seemed to take his looks too seriously, one way or another. Life came easy to Dylan, but because he was both honest and kind, people forgave him for having it better than most. Mothers might consider him a threat to their daughters' good names, until they realized that faith and convictions were not just words to him, but principles by which he lived. He often spoke up in defense of his little sister. She, in turn, loved her older brother to distraction.

"A good heart is worth more than all the smarts in the whole world," Dylan went on, giving Bethan a look that thanked her again for the morning wake-up that had spared him his mother's wrath.

"Maybe so, but it wouldn't hurt to have her do better in school," their mother replied candidly, then gestured at Bethan's plate. "You'll be cleaning that plate before you rise from the table, child. I declare, you don't eat enough to keep a sparrow alive."

———— 🌿 ————

"He's really growing, isn't he?" Bethan said with her happiest grin, lifting her face beyond the reach of the eager tongue. One hand kept the puppy at bay while the other stroked the smooth-coated back. No spine protruded through the silky hair now. The puppy had filled out with daily feeding by Mr. Russel and generous scraps from the two girls. "He's getting fat," Bethan added with a pleased giggle.

"Told you Mr. Russel would be good for him," Jodie reminded her.

Bethan turned her attention to Jodie. It was still difficult for her to believe that Jodie Harland was her very own, very best friend. But it was true. Their friendship had grown like the mongrel who had brought them together. It was a wonder to Bethan that Jodie, who could have just about any friend she wanted, seemed as pleased about their friendship as she was. "You sure did," Bethan said. "And you were right."

Jodie reached out a hand to the puppy, and the two girls stroked the wriggling body. "He sure does squirm a lot."

"That's cause he's glad to see us," Bethan replied.

"Maybe he's just glad to get our scraps," Jodie, the realist, answered.

But Bethan was quick to note, "He hasn't even eaten the scraps yet, see? They're still right where we put them. It's us he's glad to see."

"He needs a name," Jodie announced. "We can't just keep calling him Puppy." She inspected the squirming mutt. "He's growing so fast we'll soon have to call him Dog."

"Do you think Mr. Russel will let us name him?" Bethan wondered.

"Let's ask."

"But he's not here." Mr. Russel was almost always home when the girls called. Sometimes he even had a treat to share. But today their knock had not been answered. "Maybe he went into town."

"He doesn't like to go alone. He can't see well enough. Last spring he tripped on a curb and took an awful fall. Needed six stitches, Daddy said."

"Well, then, he must be somewhere." Bethan rose to her feet, the puppy doing a little dance about her gingham skirts.

"Maybe he's back in his garden. Momma says she doesn't know what he'd do without his plants. He spends hours looking after them."

Bethan was puzzled. "If his eyes are so bad, how can

he know the weeds from the good plants?"

"He has a little hoe. It's got this short handle, and he crawls along on his knees, right down the rows. He can see a little bit. But he has to get right down close and feel them with his fingers. Momma's sure he has seeing fingers." Jodie jumped up and hurried from the porch. "He smells them, too. I've seen him. He just leans right over and sniffs."

Jodie was on the path leading around the little house. But Bethan hated to leave. The puppy was kept on a short tether, and already it sensed their departure and started to whine.

"What about—" Bethan started but halted at the sight of Mr. Russel shuffling around the house. He would have bumped into the scurrying Jodie if she had not jumped out of his way. Sure enough, he had a stubby-handled hoe in his hands. It looked like a child's toy, except for the well-worn metal blade.

"That you, gals?"

"Yessir," Jodie said, skipping along beside the old man. "We just brought the puppy some scraps."

Mr. Russel chuckled. "You're gonna have that little fellow so fat he won't even be able to waddle. Sherman don't have the sense to know when to stop eating."

Both girls stopped cold. Jodie was the first to recover. "What did you say?"

"I said we gotta be careful how much we feed little Sherman." The old man mounted the steps to his porch, hand on the railing for guidance. He felt his way to his favorite chair and lowered himself into the shade. He reached into a rear pocket and retrieved a faded checkered square which he used to wipe the sweat from his brow. "Gonna have him waddling around here like a piglet, we don't watch out."

The puppy pushed himself against the elderly man's knee, his tail wagging so fiercely his whole body responded. Bethan felt a little pang at the realization that really and truly this was Mr. Russel's dog. The puppy was showing first loyalty to the old man, who had even gone and named him. Bethan swallowed around her disappointment and said faintly, "Sherman's a fine name."

"He's taken a notion to chasing the alley cats," Mr. Russel went on, clearly not having heard Bethan. "Haven't you, boy? That's why I have to tether him when I'm not right here with him. Don't want him getting an eye scratched. Those cats can be mighty mean."

Jodie stirred. "I guess we better go, Bethan."

"Lots of good company, this here little pup," Mr. Russel went on, lifting the wiggling bundle onto his lap. "You couldn't have brought me a nicer gift, little lady. No siree. Don't know what I'd do without him. He's gonna make a fine dog, too. Aren't you, Sherman?"

"Today's our last day before school starts," Jodie said, pitching her voice louder. "We're gonna go have a little picnic."

"Best be off then," said Mr. Russel, giving them a fine smile. "Sure is a grand thing, being young. You be sure and enjoy every minute of what God's given you."

Bethan echoed Jodie's goodbyes but could scarcely wait until they were out of range to demand, "What kind of name is Sherman for a dog?"

"A fine name, just like you said," Jodie replied firmly. "A war name from an old soldier."

"War name?" Bethan questioned.

"Mr. Russel fought in The War between the States, remember?"

"So?"

31

"So Sherman was a general in the war. An important one."

It was news to Bethan. But she did not read her history books with Jodie's appetite for knowledge. For a moment she envied Jodie and all the exciting information she had. Reading was so hard, especially when she had to concentrate to keep that wayward eye from straying. Her Bible study was about all the reading she could manage, other than assigned schoolwork. But in truth, it was not the reading that troubled her just then; it was the fact that Sherman was without a doubt Mr. Russel's dog.

Then she remembered all the pleasure she had seen on the elderly man's face and knew that somehow, even when the disappointment cut at her, it was right.

Bethan breathed a deep sigh and hurried to keep up. She had to agree with Jodie after all—Sherman was a fine name for the old gentleman's dog.

———— 🌿 ————

From the hillside they could look out over the bordering pines and see the church steeple. It was a reassuring sight, as they were fairly certain that if they were to actually ask permission, neither of their mothers would have allowed them to wander so far. But both girls loved the hillside meadow, although for different reasons. Bethan loved the flowers and the sweet smell and the cooling breeze, not to mention the excitement of having some place which was theirs and theirs alone. Jodie loved that as well, but mostly she loved the grand view and the closeness of the sky. The world's borders were much bigger up on the hillside than down in Harmony, and tomorrow seemed much closer at hand.

An old picnic hamper, missing one of the lids and thus designated as ideal by the girls, was covered by a patched kitchen towel. A small tea set of real china, Jodie's Christmas present from two years back, was set up on the remaining lid. They sipped fresh cider and munched cookies from Moira's kitchen.

Their refreshment completed, the girls settled on the bank surrounded by wildflowers and knee-high grass. Bethan looked up from the daisy chain she was forming to study Jodie's progress. It was just as she thought. Jodie's chain was already longer than her own. Nor did Jodie have trouble getting the loops to stay together. Bethan's own chain kept coming apart at the links.

Bethan sighed and went back to carefully maneuvering the stems into place, the tip of her tongue barely showing between pursed lips.

Lifting her chain in the air, Jodie broke the silence. "Look," she invited proudly, rising to her feet. "It's three feet long."

Bethan raised her eyes. "Not three feet," she dared to dispute softly. "Three feet would touch the ground."

"Well, two feet," Jodie responded stubbornly. "Almost three feet."

Bethan nodded silently. Maybe it was. She wasn't sure.

Jodie settled back beside Bethan and declared, "Your eye's getting better."

Bethan winced inwardly. She hated having people talk about her weak eye.

"Bet it'll be perfectly acceptable soon," Jodie went on.

Perfectly acceptable was one of Jodie's new expressions. Bethan thought Jodie was in danger of wearing it out. Almost everything that summer had been either perfectly acceptable or totally deplorable.

Bethan worked another loop and said nothing.

But Jodie seemed oblivious to Bethan's discomfort about the topic. "Do you still have to wear the patch?"

"Almost every evening and a lot of other times at home," Bethan admitted quietly. "I hate it."

"Well, I think it's getting better," Jodie said, reaching for another daisy. "You hardly notice the turning anymore."

"Doc Franklin doesn't think it is," Bethan said, revealing part of her very worst fear. "He wants Momma to make me wear it all the time. Even at school."

Jodie stopped her looping. The seriousness of her expression told Bethan that Jodie understood what wearing it all the time would mean. Already the kids loved to make fun of Bethan, at least when Jodie was not around to defend her. To make her wear the hated eyepatch at school would be disastrous.

Jodie returned to her work with a snort. "What does old Doc Franklin know anyway? I say it's getting better, and that's final."

In spite of herself, Bethan smiled. It was good to have a friend like Jodie. Very good.

They worked on in silence, each deep in thought. At length Bethan dared to voice her most secret concern. She had never discussed it with anyone before. Not even with Jodie. "Do you think—" Bethan hesitated, then hurried on, "Do you think a man might want to . . . to marry me, even with my eye?"

Jodie looked surprised. "If he didn't, he'd be a dolt," she responded hotly, using one of her more colorful descriptions.

This was good news for Bethan. She very much wanted to believe Jodie's declaration.

But Jodie continued to stare at her. "Do you really want to get married?"

Bethan was shocked. "Of course." All girls wanted to marry. It was part of becoming—well, a proper young lady. If she didn't marry, what else could she do? Become a spinster? Spinsters were talked about behind discreet hands, even if they did make fine librarians or teachers.

"I might not get married," Jodie stated.

Something in Jodie's tone told Bethan her friend had given this a lot of thought. "Why ever not?"

Jodie carefully fastened the next loop in her chain. "If you get married, you have to do what your husband wants," she said frankly.

"So?" That was simply the way things were.

"I don't want somebody else telling me what to do with my life," replied Jodie. "I want to chart my own course, make my own path, be my own person, like Miss Charles says I should."

Yes, Bethan reminded herself. Miss Charles certainly said things like that, though Bethan had never really understood just what the teacher meant by those statements.

Jodie's dark eyes gleamed. "I'll have her as my main teacher this year. Isn't that great?"

"I guess so." Bethan was not as taken with the new teacher and her wise words as Jodie seemed to be. Teachers were not high on Bethan's list of favorite people—maybe because she didn't feel like she was high on theirs. Besides, Miss Charles was already old. Probably close to forty or at least thirty, and she wasn't even married.

"I think she is so wonderful!" Jodie enthused. "She says, with my intelligence I can be anything I want if I just put my mind to it. She thinks I should be a teacher. But I want to be something different."

"Like what?" Bethan challenged, forgetting about her chain and letting it get entangled in her lap.

"I think," Jodie said, a faraway look on her face, "I'd like to be a scientist."

"Ladies don't become scientists," Bethan said emphatically.

"Some ladies do," Jodie shot back.

"Not . . . not in Harmony, not in North Carolina."

For a moment Jodie seemed at a loss, then her chin lifted stubbornly. "Then I'll be the first," she said firmly.

Seeing the determined look in Jodie's eyes, Bethan felt sorry she had let their talk develop into an argument. "You can be a scientist if you want to," she conceded, then added softly, "if they let you."

For one moment Jodie's eyes became even darker at the challenge. But her expression softened when she looked at Bethan. "What about you? Don't *you* have dreams?"

"You mean at night? Sure."

"No, silly. Not sleepy dreams—*dreams*. For the future."

Bethan shrugged. "I don't know." Then she brightened. "Sure. Have a nice husband and raise a nice family."

Impatiently Jodie dropped the daisy chain to the ground beside her. "But what else?"

"Why does there have to be something else? It's the nicest dream I know." Bethan looked out over the village, wondering why it was so hard to make her best friend understand. "I do think about it sometimes. Well, a lot, I guess. I wonder which of the fellows we know might . . . might fall in love with me and ask me to marry him." She showed Jodie her dimples. "I hope he's nice—so I'll love him back."

"Listen, you don't need to marry one of the dolts

from here—even if you do only get married. You could marry anybody. All you need to do is get that eye of yours fixed up, and you'd be the most beautiful girl in town."

Jodie looked so sure of what she was saying that for one moment it was almost easy for Bethan to believe her. "You really think so?"

"You ought to find yourself somebody special," Jodie assured her with conviction.

Then Bethan's courage wilted, as always happened when someone talked about how she looked. "Somebody who loves me *will* be special," she said, her voice now quiet and subdued as she stared out at the town below.

But when she looked back at her friend, she saw Jodie was not listening. She too gazed out over the horizon. "I'm going to do something exciting with my life, just you wait and see. I'll be somebody who goes places and does things, like Miss Charles says."

"But you can't," Bethan protested.

"Why ever not?" Jodie bristled.

"You're going to be a lady," Bethan pleaded. "And you're my best friend."

"I can be a lady and your friend and still be anything I want."

"But what if . . . what if it takes you away from here?"

"That's exactly what I want. To go out and have adventures and see places."

"But what about me?" Bethan wailed.

"You'll marry a rich man who's famous, and you'll have a big house in some *fabulous* city—maybe in the same city where I will be living—and have servants and furs and flowers and a shiny new automobile and—"

"I don't care about any of those things," Bethan protested. "All I want is to be a good Christian and to find a good man to be my husband and have a family, and I'll be happy. And I don't *ever* want to leave Harmony."

Jodie stopped. "I don't understand you, Bethan Keane."

"And I don't understand you, Jodie Harland."

They looked at each other in utter confusion.

CHAPTER THREE

THE INSTANT JODIE AWOKE, her heart was racing with excitement. Today was her first all-school spelling bee, and tomorrow started Thanksgiving holidays! Two of the very best things in the world coming together at once. It was almost more than she could bear.

She slid from the bed, pulled the flannel nightie over her head, folded it and placed it under her pillow, then moved across the wooden floor with its scattering of braided rugs to start her morning wash. It took both hands to lift the big white pitcher with the blue ring around the top. In spite of her carefulness, the water sloshed onto the old chiffarobe as she poured it into the bowl. Bowl and pitcher were chipped from generations of use, the glazing spotted with age, but Jodie had never stopped to think about the imperfections. She splashed her face, breathing in the sweet scent of morning.

Humming an excited little tune, she dressed and brushed her dark hair only because her mother would notice if she came down for breakfast without having done so. Her mother always noticed the small things. Her father seemed to notice nothing. Her mother would take one look at her, see whether her face was washed and the thick brown locks brushed, and if not send her back up to do double the strokes. Somehow she even seemed to know when Jodie did less than the required fifty.

Jodie did not like her face. Which was probably why she did not like any small chore that meant looking into her mirror. She felt her features were too sharp. All planes and angles, her mother had once said, and then smiled away the comment and took her off for a sweet and a cream soda as well. Her mother, Louise Harland, was both comforting and intelligent, which to Jodie's mind was a very special combination.

Her impatient strokes at her hair slowed as her mind went back to a conversation with Bethan the day before. As they had walked to school together, Jodie had asked, "What do you think is the most important thing in the world?"

Bethan was slow in replying. "You always seem to ask such strange questions."

"I'm just wondering." She passed her satchel of books to her other hand. "What do you think is absolutely indispensable?"

Bethan shrugged, clearly unsure exactly what the word meant. "How could you ever pick one thing?"

"I could," Jodie announced. "I think it's *words*."

Bethan stared at her. "Words?"

Jodie felt triumphant, as though she had just discovered one of life's great secrets. "Think what it would be like if we didn't have words. We couldn't talk to each other. We couldn't learn about things. We couldn't tell each other how to do something or read about it. We'd be lost. Totally devastated." She walked a few steps farther before concluding, "That's why it's so crucial to be a good reader."

"I'm finding all sorts of hard words in the Bible,"

Bethan acknowledged slowly. "I try and try, but I can't seem to learn all the words I need. Why can't we use the easy ones?"

"The easy ones don't always say it exactly right," Jodie answered, sparking with enthusiasm.

"Words are important," Bethan conceded. "But I think there are other things even bigger."

Jodie stopped and looked at Bethan. Her friend did not often challenge Jodie's comments. "Like what?"

"Like God," Bethan said, her voice soft yet firm.

Jodie shook her head vehemently. "God's a *person*. I'm not talking about *persons*. I'm talking about *things*."

But Bethan was not put off so easily. "But *faith*, how we live and talk to God. That's a thing."

Jodie gave her an all-knowing look and countered smugly, "You couldn't have told me that, not without words."

Yet now as she stood before the mirror, Jodie found herself wondering whether people or things were most important.

She gave her head a little shake, shrugged, and hurried down the stairs and into the kitchen. "Good morning, Daddy."

Her father looked up absently from his paper long enough to give his only child a distracted smile. "Did you sleep well?"

"Yes, sir." She watched him nod and return to his paper and wondered if he really heard her at all. One day she was going to announce something like she'd fought dragons all night long and see if all he did was nod and return to his reading.

Jodie should have been used to it. She already was old enough to understand that Parker Harland was naturally a silent man, quiet and reserved with all except his wife. Her momma was the only person who could draw him out. Not even Jodie could find a way to hold her father's attention for long.

Jodie did love her father, though she didn't feel that she knew him well. She knew some things about him, but it was her mother who had given her the information. Both sets of grandparents had emigrated from Switzerland. Her parents had been born and raised right here in Harmony, growing up with the town. Parker had left only long enough to take his chemist's training up north, then had returned as quickly as possible. He was the town's only druggist, and owned the Harland Apothecary. He took his work very seriously. Whenever he was not at work or reading the papers brought in by train from Raleigh, he was busy perusing the scientific journals which he kept stacked on the living room shelves. The only time Jodie had with her father was their occasional walks on a Sunday afternoon, and even then her father seldom spoke. But she knew that in his own quiet way he loved her.

Jodie found her mother to be a very different person. Where her father was strong and solid and silent, her mother was lithe and slender. And very often ill. Jodie knew it was her mother's health that had not allowed them to have another child, although Jodie had often thought it would be nice to have a baby brother or a sister. Jodie had once heard her mother tell a neighbor that the good Lord had granted her a double helping of joy in the one daughter, since He would not allow her more. Jodie recalled those words whenever she felt a little lonely in their big rambling house.

When she was feeling well, Louise loved to sing. Jodie could always tell when her mother was having a bad day, because those were the times when she returned from school to a quiet home. Otherwise her mother was either humming about her chores or chatting with a neighbor or playing hymns on the high-back piano which stood in the parlor. The only disappointment Louise Harland had ever expressed over her daughter was Jodie's seeming lack of interest in anything musical. Except, of course, for the pleasure she took in her mother's singing, occasionally even humming along quietly to herself. And Jodie was not the only one who enjoyed her mother's happy bearing. Louise Harland cast joy over her husband's quiet moods like sunshine dispelling mountain shadows.

Noting gladly the brief snatch of a hymn from her mother, Jodie's thoughts returned to the day ahead.

"Incongruous," she exclaimed, kissing her mother's cheek. "Definitely incongruous."

"My, but if you don't gobble up words like other children do sweets," Louise declared proudly. "Did you hear that, Parker?"

"Yes, yes," her father mumbled, shaking out the paper's next page.

But her mother made up for her father's lack of enthusiasm. "You said it just right. Now can you use it in a sentence?"

"It is incongruous how I am so excited about school and the spelling bee today, and then plan to do—well, do nothing all day with Bethan tomorrow," Jodie announced.

"I could not agree more," Louise said with a laugh. "And now, my incongruous child, sit yourself down at the table and have your breakfast."

Jodie half skipped, half ran to the corner dominated

by the old maple. It was the grandest tree in all Harmony, a great leafy canopy which spread out over the joining of the two main streets. A half-dozen grown men would have trouble joining hands about its trunk. At present, the tree was crowned by a grand dome of autumn colors, burnished red and orange and copper in the morning light. All the town knew the place as Tree Corner, and it was where Jodie and Bethan met every morning for the walk to school.

This morning, however, there was no undersized copper-haired beauty coming down the lane toward her. In fact, Jodie waited so long she almost decided Bethan was sick, and was ready to start off alone when she spotted the little figure walking slowly toward her. Even at that distance, Jodie could see the dragging footsteps and sorrowful cast to the shoulders. Jodie raced down the street, only to stop when Bethan's face raised from beneath the bright veil of hair.

The eyepatch was strapped into place.

"Oh, Bethan," Jodie said, the sorrow in her voice matching the expression in the face before her.

"Momma says I've got to," her friend mumbled miserably. "Doctor Franklin too."

"But you've been so good."

Bethan's visible eye leaked a single tear. "They say it's not improving. They say if I don't use it, it might get so bad I'll go blind in that eye."

Jodie bit off further argument. Anyone with a heart could see wearing the patch made Bethan miserable. For one moment Jodie thought of reaching out and undoing the strings. They could put it back in place on their way home from school. But even as Jodie considered it, she realized that Moira Keane was an intelligent woman and also a good mother. Jodie knew instinctively the woman ached for her little girl and would not have taken such a decision lightly. What Bethan needed was support and strength, not a conspirator.

"Well, that's that, then," Jodie said briskly. "You've got to do whatever it takes to make this thing go away once and for all."

Bethan fingered the triangular patch. It was black and stiff and covered with shiny silk. The black strings crossed her forehead, pinching the hair in tight above both ears, before tying into an unattractive bow at the back. On her delicate features the patch looked bulky and horrid. Bethan said quietly, "I hate it."

Jodie made an innocent face. "Hate what?"

Bethan stared at Jodie without responding, then said, "You know—this eyepatch."

Jodie scrunched up her face and made a pretend search of Bethan's peaches-and-cream features. "What eyepatch? I don't see anything."

"Oh, you." Bethan swung her books in an arc, and Jodie leaped out of the way in exaggerated fashion. Bethan managed a small smile.

"That's better," Jodie said, grabbing Bethan's free arm and pulling her forward. "Now we have to hurry, and I do mean hurry. I can't get in Miss Charles' bad books today. I've got a spelling bee to win."

———— ✿ ————

Despite their best efforts, they were late anyway. Or at least Jodie was. She insisted on walking Bethan down to her class, and gave the room a cold stare as whispers and snickers began over Bethan's eyepatch. To anyone else, the patch would have been an irritation. For Bethan, it was a crushing blow. She was so quiet, and so sensitive. Jodie picked out the three worst class bullies, singled them out for a warning glower, one at a time, and strode meaningfully from the room. Anyone who made trouble for her best friend could count on big trouble from her.

Because of her self-imposed detour, she was scurrying down the hall to her own class minutes after the morning bell had rung. Jodie saw Miss Charles up ahead, deep in conversation with Mrs. Fitzgerald, and her heart sank. There was no way around the two teachers. She stopped where she was and hoped with all her heart that neither teacher would cast a glance her way.

"I'm still not sure it's a good idea," Miss Charles was saying.

"Me neither," Mrs. Fitzgerald agreed. "I hate the thought of holding a student back. Especially someone as tenderhearted as little Bethan."

Even before she realized it, Jodie started forward at the sound of Bethan's name. The two women remained so engrossed in their discussion they did not take any notice of her approach.

Though Miss Amanda Charles was already in her second year of teaching at the Harmony school, Mrs. Fitzgerald had just joined the school. She had been assigned the class of slower learners, while Miss Charles taught the brighter students. These two new teachers were a generation younger than any of the others, which Jodie supposed was why they had quickly become fast friends. She liked them both.

She watched now as Miss Charles bit her lip in agitation, then asked, "You're sure she can't keep up?"

"That's just it," Mrs. Fitzgerald replied. "She is so shy, it's hard to tell what is her real potential. But she is struggling."

"She's also quite small for her age," Miss Charles commented reflectively. "Perhaps she would be more comfortable with the younger children. Maybe you are right."

"No!" The exclamation was out before Jodie could help herself. She stepped forward, then stopped abruptly as the two teachers turned her way. Her face flushed with her brashness, but she swallowed, took a deep breath, and lifted her chin in determination, even if it did mean getting herself in trouble. "I mean, please, you can't," she continued in a quieter voice, almost pleading in its tone. "That won't help her at all."

"What are you doing out here in the hall?" Miss Charles demanded, giving Jodie a rather stern look.

"I was just . . ." Jodie waved a vague hand back in the direction of Bethan's class.

"This is not the type of example I would expect from my best pupil," Miss Charles said, her tone serious.

But Jodie refused to retreat, even if she got in further trouble. "Please, you can't hold her back. You just can't. She's got a problem with her eye already. She'll be humiliated."

Miss Charles looked to the other teacher. "What problem is this?"

"A lazy eye. There's a scientific name for it, but blessed if I can remember it," explained Mrs. Fitzgerald.

"Amblyopia," Jodie offered. "I looked it up. It is usually a correctable condition."

The two women looked at her askance. Even Miss Charles seemed at times uncertain just how to deal with Jodie. Only the week before Jodie had heard Mrs. Sloane, Kirsten's mother, call her an upstart. Miss Charles had come to her rescue, though, and said it was simply the

sign of a brilliant mind, to run where others were forced to walk.

Jodie went on with her explanation. "Her eye isn't getting better. Yet. So she has to wear this eyepatch sometimes. And she hates it."

Mrs. Fitzgerald nodded slowly. "Wearing a patch would be difficult for any child—but for Bethan . . ." Her voice trailed off.

The pleading tone returned. "It would just crush her to have to stay back," Jodie said. "Please. I can help her with her studies at night. She's smart. Really. I know she can do the work."

Miss Charles' gaze softened. "You would offer your time? Why?"

Jodie nodded and replied simply, "She's my very best friend."

Jodie caught up with Bethan before the spelling bee. She was walking down the hallway as close to the wall as she could manage, a little waif with her books clutched close to her chest. Her face was a mask of misery, the patch a glowering shadow on her delicate features. Jodie's heart twisted at the sight of so much sadness on her friend's face. She walked over with as big a smile as she could muster up. "I was looking for you. I've just had the best idea."

"What?" Bethan's voice was barely above a whisper.

Jodie fell into step beside her friend. "I think we ought to meet in the evening and do our homework together," she said. "Every night. I could help you with any hard stuff."

Bethan made a face. "I'd only slow you down."

"No, you wouldn't. Besides, I'm two weeks ahead on my own assignments anyway."

Bethan walked awhile in reflective silence before admitting, "That would be really nice."

"Sure, we all can use help from time to time." Jodie gave her brightest smile. "Then it's settled. We'll start tonight. It'll be a lot of fun."

Bethan's sad little face tasted a tiny smile. "That'd be different. School and fun don't fit together in my mind."

"You'll see." A sudden idea struck Jodie so hard she had to stop and take a breath. "Do you have another of those eyepatches?"

"Yes." The mask of misery settled back into place. "Momma makes me carry a spare. She says getting this one dirty or lost is no excuse to stop wearing it."

Jodie held out her hand. "Let me borrow it for a while, okay?"

Bethan dug into her pocket and handed it over. "Why?"

"Oh, just something I thought of." Jodie backed away. "I've got to run. See you after the contest."

Bethan reached for Jodie's arm. "I heard one of the older girls say she was going to turn you to mincemeat."

Jodie snorted in disdain. "I know how to spell words she's never even heard of before," she boasted, though inwardly she felt a flutter of nerves.

"Sure you do." Bethan gave her the first real smile of the day. "Good luck."

Jodie waved and ran off.

She entered the school's main hall, where the youngest students were taught in one large class. One end was raised to a stubby stage. Slowly she proceeded to the small area behind the stage where one student from each class was gathered. Jodie didn't mind the glances cast her way. She already knew the talk going around, that she was that young know-it-all, the one to beat this year. She turned her back on them and walked over to the rear window, using the reflection to tie the eyepatch in place.

The image was distorted and vague. Even so, the sight of the black triangle masking one eye was enough to make her step back in dismay. It was so . . . so *noticeable*. Jodie quailed for a moment but stiffened with resolve. This was something she had to do.

Bethan would know for sure and for certain that she did not need to go through this alone.

CHAPTER FOUR

JODIE RAN DOWN the street, enjoying the freedom of a spring afternoon without homework or chores, when she spotted her friend up ahead. Bethan scurried toward the corner, her eyes nervously watching the darkening sky. One hand clutched a brown paper sack. Jodie hurried after her. "Bethan—wait!"

Bethan turned to wait while Jodie came running up to join her. Jodie stopped for breath and demanded, "Where are you going?"

Bethan held up the sack. "I'm taking these to feed Sherman." The puppy taken in by Mr. Russel, the old soldier, had now grown into a handsome crossbreed, large enough to send the girls sprawling with his playfulness if they weren't careful. "Momma says I can save him scraps, long as I don't let them go rancid in her kitchen."

Jodie could just imagine. Rancid in the Keane household meant anything that had been left out for more than an hour or two after mealtime. "I'll go with you. I haven't seen Sherman in a couple of weeks."

"He's really growing," Bethan announced and resumed her hurried errand. "Mr. Russel takes real good care of him. And he's even teaching him stuff."

Jodie had to stretch out her legs to keep up. "Like what?"

"Well, he can't roll over or anything like that. Not yet. But Mr. Russel's got him so he doesn't chew on his slippers anymore. And he doesn't try to pull all the slip rugs off the floor." Bethan tripped along the lane, almost running in her haste. "Mr. Russel says he's in a hurry to teach him some manners, since Sherman's shooting up so fast. He says Sherman's got to learn not to greet everybody he likes with two great paws in the center of their chest."

Jodie, puffing a little from the pace, said, "Do we have to go so fast?"

Bethan lifted her eyes to the sky. Jodie knew the approaching clouds were bothering her. Bethan was more than a little uncomfortable about storms. The loud cracks of thunder and flashes of ragged lightning always made her friend nervous, despite her stated belief that God would care for her in all circumstances. It was one thing to hear those words in Sunday school, and another thing entirely to put them to the test out of doors.

"Momma says I need to be back before it rains. She even told me not to stop to play with Sherman, or visit with Mr. Russel. Just take the scraps in and get my body on home."

Jodie could almost hear Bethan's mother saying the words. Her own steps quickened to keep up. "You're not wearing your eyepatch."

Bethan had the ability to sigh with all her body. "I *have* been wearing it."

Jodie felt the tug in her heart at all the sadness those words contained. "Will you have to wear it to school again?"

Bethan nodded solemnly. "If Momma says I must."

Jodie's brow furrowed. For one short hour, she had understood Bethan's pain and embarrassment. When she had appeared on stage for the spelling bee wearing Bethan's eyepatch, none of the others had dared tease her, but she had heard the snickers, seen the snide looks being exchanged and felt the trauma of being a spectacle. It had been one of the most difficult moments of her entire life. Even so, she would not let her friend down. "The next time you have to wear it to school," she offered, "bring the spare one for me."

But Bethan shook her head. "You don't need to do that," she said. "Honest. I really did appreciate you standing up for me like you did. But—"

Jodie cut in. "I'll wear it every time you do."

"No," Bethan said quickly and followed up with a smile. There was something about the way Bethan could smile that seemed to lift her small frame right off the earth. It twisted Jodie's heart so, as though suddenly her friend were no longer tied by years or school or anything else Jodie knew and understood. As though somehow she had grown in ways denied to Jodie, and almost everyone else. "No," Bethan repeated. "It's okay now."

"I don't see how, if you've still got to wear the thing."

"Don't you see, it's like you changed everything by what you did. Doing it more isn't so important now. It's almost like," she scrunched up her forehead with the effort to explain, "it's like you made them all see themselves in the eyepatch. Momma says it was the kindest thing you could have ever done for me."

A loud crack of thunder caused them both to jump and look upward. The menacing clouds had moved in quickly and now boiled directly above them.

53

"C'mon," cried Jodie, whirling about and reaching for Bethan's hand.

"We'll never make it either home or to Mr. Russel's before it strikes," Bethan argued.

"Well, at least we can reach Tree Corner."

A flash of lightning lit up the darkening sky, followed by a loud clap of thunder. Bethan did not need further encouragement. Clutching to the brown bag tightly with one hand and Jodie with the other, she ran as fast as she could for the shelter of the grand maple tree.

They ducked under the protective branches just as the rain arrived. Straight down it came, encircling them in a sheer curtain of water. It seemed as though the sky were determined to empty every cloud at once. The girls wrapped arms around each other and pressed themselves up closely against the trunk. Faint gusts blew dampness over them, and occasional drops made their way through the great tree's protection. The rain dripped upon their heads, but even the wetness assured them the old tree would protect them from the worst of the storm. Even so, each rumble brought another shiver through Bethan's body.

Jodie searched for something to take Bethan's mind from the thunder and settled on, "Have you read the history lesson for tomorrow?"

Bethan nodded and shivered at the same time. "I didn't understand it, though. I mean, why did they have to fight the Civil War?"

"Because," Jodie said matter-of-factly, "President Lincoln didn't want Americans to own slaves."

"No, no, that's what they *disagreed* about," Bethan said. "But why did they have to *fight* about it."

Jodie slackened her hold on both Bethan and the tree so she could move back a half-pace. Bethan had the habit of asking the strangest questions when they studied together. "It's just like the book says," she answered. "They fought to make the slaves free."

"But couldn't they have just sat down and talked about it? Why did they have to take guns and go out killing each other?" She seemed to have forgotten the storm. "Think of all the soldiers and mothers and children, Jodie. Their homes burned up and there were guns and bullets and people being hurt—the book said after the war there wasn't enough to eat. Why didn't they get together and discuss it and pray about it?"

"Maybe they did," Jodie countered. "President Lincoln believed in God. That's why he thought owning slaves was all wrong."

"General Lee believed in God too. So why didn't they let God work out the problem?" Bethan demanded. "God could have let the slaves go free without the fighting and the hurting. I know He could."

Jodie turned and stared out at the departing storm. Bethan's questions often left her grappling for answers. She watched as the rain gradually lessened, heard the thunder rolling pleasantly in the distance, and wondered what on earth she should say. The assignment and the readings had all seemed so clear to her until Bethan had started in.

"I sure don't know exactly what God would have done," Bethan persisted. "But I think He would have figured it all out, and without hurting all those folks. They just didn't give Him time."

Jodie had opened her mouth to reply when she spotted a figure hurrying toward them. She pointed and exclaimed, "That's Momma!"

They raced out from under cover toward Louise Harland. She had clearly not fared as well as the girls. Her clothing, soaked and clinging, hung about her. And she was shivering so hard she could scarcely get out the words, "What on earth are you two doing out in this storm?"

"Bethan had some scraps for Sherman, but the storm stopped us." Jodie inspected her mother. "You're all wet."

"I'm well aware of that, child." Louise flapped out her dress. "I took a few things over to Mr. Russel and got caught precisely halfway home. The sky was clear as a bell when I left. I didn't think of taking a parasol." She looked the two girls over and demanded, "Why aren't you very wet?"

Jodie pointed behind her. "We hid under the maple."

"Oh, you mustn't do that. Not ever." Louise turned them both around and started down the street. Her teeth chattered as she continued, "Never take refuge under a tree when there is lightning, daughter. Lightning might . . . but never mind that."

"I never fed Sherman," Bethan protested.

"Well," Louise inspected the two girls. "Neither of you got all that wet. Mind the puddles and keep your feet dry. And be home in half an hour."

"No dawdling," Bethan agreed. "I already promised my mother."

"All right." Jodie's mother managed a smile. "Now I really must be off. I can already feel a chill setting in."

"Just put them on the bed there, that's a dear."

With a relieved sigh, Jodie set the packages on the foot of her parents' big four-poster bed. Even though

Easter was still two weeks away, already the days were sweltering. All of March had been unseasonably hot, especially coming as it had after such a cold winter. Up and down Main Street, Jodie and her mother had passed clusters of farmers and city merchants arguing over whether or not to go ahead and plant early, possibly risking it all to a late freeze. Being raised in a country town, Jodie did not need to be told that the earliest harvesters reaped the greatest profits.

Although Jodie really did not much care what she wore, shopping for clothes with her mother was not a chore but an adventure. Louise Harland was known and appreciated by all the store clerks in Harmony. Which meant that while her mother received the best possible service, Jodie was usually treated to a candy or sometimes even a soda.

Her mother never objected to these little gifts, nor did she tell Jodie to watch what she ate so it didn't spoil her appetite, like Bethan's mother did when the four went out together. Louise Harland would often chuckle at Moira and say, "Leave the child alone, Moira. We're indulging ourselves; why shouldn't they?" Moira would subside after that, but Jodie could tell that for Bethan a little of the joy was already taken from the treat. Jodie was very glad she had a mother who understood how to have a good time.

Jodie did not need to be told what to do after putting the purchases on the bed. It was part of their little shopping ritual. She began laying out all the various items. Her mother was going to be bridesmaid for a longtime friend whose first husband had died several years back, and who was now getting married again. Louise Harland had said it was pure silliness, a woman of her age playing bridesmaid—or was it bridesmatron—and marching down the aisle. But Jodie knew her mother was so excited she could hardly contain herself.

Her mother had insisted that they have matching dresses, since Jodie was to be the flower girl in the wedding. They were a deeper shade of the same color as the bridal gown, which Louise had repeatedly explained was not under any circumstances going to be white. Jodie had heard several people say it was only Louise's good sense which was keeping the entire proceedings from being an utter shambles. She did not understand what they meant but was pleased to hear her mother being praised.

The dresses had come from Landon's, which everyone said had goods as fine as any to be found in Raleigh. In spite of Jodie's lack of interest in clothes, she did think they were beautiful. And Louise's practical nature planned that they would do double-duty as Easter dresses. They were the loveliest shade of pink, with pale gray trim and mother-of-pearl buttons. Even though they had brought the dresses home once before to try them with shoes and hats and handbags, and had worn them through a half-dozen fittings, this was different. The dresses were theirs now.

Jodie smoothed a crease, wondering if she would look as grown up as she felt, wearing the same dress as her mother. She went to the closet to fetch the shoes and hats and lay them alongside. She turned, smiling, to her mother for approval on her accomplishment, but what she saw made her heart skip a beat. "What's wrong, Momma?"

"Just a little headache." Louise rubbed her temples with two middle fingers. Her eyes were closed so tightly that lines ran all the way across her forehead. "I must have tired myself out more than I thought." She slowly eased herself onto the nearest chair.

Jodie felt a faint cold fear tug at her chest. Her mother's complexion had suddenly gone pale. "Do you want me to get your medicine?"

"Thank you, dear. Maybe that would be a good idea." Louise tried for a smile, but the fact that she could not manage to open her eyes spoiled the effect. "Parker is always saying my shopping will be the death of me. Maybe he's right after all."

"Don't even joke like that," Jodie tossed over her shoulder as she raced into the bathroom, climbed on the little stool, and opened the heavy mirrored door. The brown bottle with the oddly shaped glass stopper was there on the top shelf. Jodie knew the label from memory, as she did many of the medicines in her father's store. It read, "Doctor Pitt's Laudanum Mixture and Headache Relief." Beside it was a clear flask which read, "Witch Hazel Liniment." Her mother sometimes took a half-spoonful of the liniment in juice, saying it did not confuse her head quite as much as the other. Jodie pulled down both bottles and scurried back. "Which do you want, Momma?"

"I think perhaps I will have to . . ." The pinched lines across her forehead suddenly reached out to etch themselves down around her eyes and her mouth. Louise stiffened up in a spasm of pain. "Oh, dear Lord, help me."

"Momma!" Jodie tried to reach for her mother with both hands full and dropped the laudanum bottle on the hardwood floor. It broke, releasing a treacly sweet odor. Jodie did not even notice. She managed to set the other bottle down as her mother eased forward and into her arms. "What's the matter, Momma?"

"Help me to the bed." Louise's voice had suddenly gone faint. She tried to rise but could not manage it. "Help me, child."

"I'm trying." The extra weight threatened to buckle Jodie's legs as her mother gripped her shoulders and pulled herself upright, only to bend over so far she was draped across Jodie's shoulders. Louise's ribcage pressed hard upon Jodie's head. She could hear her mother's labored breathing and the little gasping moans she gave with each faltering step.

Jodie managed to half carry, half drag her mother to the bed. But once there, Louise seemed to lose the ability to move any farther on her own. Jodie tried to settle her on the high-framed bed, but Louise nearly slid to the floor. Again the girl's legs trembled with the strain of trying to keep her mother upright. Jodie turned her head toward the open window and screamed with all her might, *"Help me, someone, please help!"*

The scream seemed to bring Louise back from the verge of unconsciousness. With another low-pitched groan she found the strength to ease up and onto the bed. She fell back, the new dresses crumpling beneath her, and wrapped both hands around her temples. Jodie lifted her mother's legs one at a time to the bed, pulling off her shoes. She whimpered as she looked at the utterly inert form before her on the bed. Then she raced for the stairs, screaming for her father.

"Bethan Keane! You'll be coming in here this instant if you know what's good for you!"

Hastily, Bethan set aside the pail holding the chicken feed and scampered for the back porch. When her mother's voice took on the sharp Welsh lilt it was time to fly. "What's the matter?"

"Just you look at the sight of you. How on earth do you ever expect to grow into a proper young lady, mussed up as you are?"

"But, Momma, I was out doing the chores and you always say—"

"Never you mind what I'm always saying and not saying. Get yourself upstairs and have a good wash, behind the ears and your neck as well, mind. And put on your good Sunday dress."

Bethan hesitated. "But it's only Tuesday."

"Up the stairs with you, before I give you something to send you on your way."

Bethan did as she was told. There was no place for questions when her mother was in such a state. Bethan could not help but feel a smidgen of relief, though, as she raced for her room. At least Moira was not angry with *her*. She could tell from years of hearing her mother cover her true feelings by striking out at whoever was handy. But Bethan had no idea what had set her mother off this time.

She was back downstairs in record time. "I'm ready, Momma."

"Let's be having a look at you, then." Moira turned from the stove, where three pots were sending up great wafts of fragrant steam. "Did you wash like I told you?"

"Yes, ma'am." Bethan glanced at the simmering pots. "Are we having company?"

"That food's not for us." Moira straightened Bethan's fine lace collar she had crocheted herself, pulled her sleeves down straight, ran one hand through her daughter's hair. "You're sprouting up faster than summer corn. This time next year I'll not be looking down to you any longer."

There was a strangeness to her mother's tone now,

an urgency which caught at Bethan's own heart. "Tell me what's the matter—please, Momma."

"Your friend needs you," Moira finally replied simply, sadness deepening her gaze.

"Jodie? Something's happened to Jodie?"

"Shush now, and listen good. It's her mother that's ailing, and the daughter who's needing. You're young still, but the dear Lord has chosen this time for you to learn what it really means to be a friend." The hand traced across her forehead once more. "Don't speak unless she asks you to, mind. Jodie won't be wanting your words just now. She'll be needing your strength."

"But what—"

Two hands spun her about. "Go and be a friend. And if it's answers you're needing, or help, or strength of your own, reach out to the One who's always there."

The first thing Bethan saw when she hurried up the walk to Jodie's house was Parker Harland, hand on old Doc Franklin's arm. "Tell me it's not the influenza, John."

"Let's hope not," he hedged, turning to go down the porch steps. "But I won't lie to you, Parker. I don't like the looks of it. Not one bit."

Age and hardship and observing life's pain and sickness over the years had turned Doc Franklin into all corners and hollows. He had birthed most of the town, and he treated them with the gruffness of a favorite grandfather, rarely surprised by what they managed to get themselves into. He had the experience and ability to turn the worst of wounds into a scratch needing little more than bed rest and a bandage. Ailments were scoffed at, fevers something to be cowed with a severe lecture and aspirin. There were few within the city who did not quake before the stern old man. To have John Franklin refuse to make light of Louise's ailment turned Bethan's stomach to ice.

Doc Franklin ineffectively smoothed the unkempt thatch of graying hair with his free hand. "It's a right corker," he mused to himself, then turned back to ask Jodie's father, "Has Louise been pushing herself over-hard?"

"No harder than usual." Parker Harland's eyes held the doctor as firmly as the hand on his arm. "But she got caught in the storm the other day. Had a bad chill by the time she got home. I put her to bed with a toddy and a hot water bottle."

"A chill, did you say?" For some reason the news turned old Doc Franklin even more grave. "Well, we'll know soon enough." He turned again to the steps. "Keep the child away from her, Parker. And best you not spend any more time in the room than need be. Certainly not more than every hour or so."

"Why not?" Parker Harland refused to let the doctor go. "It's just a bad chill, maybe a chest cold. Isn't that right?"

Doc Franklin paused to look again at Jodie's father. "We've been friends and colleagues too long for lies to come between us now. What we've got in there is a lady suffering from the worst headache of her life, along with a gradually rising fever, a blistering sore throat, and se-vere nausea. Not to mention she can't remain in one po-sition for more than ten seconds at a time." Doc Franklin stared deep into the eyes of Harmony's only pharmacist and asked quietly, "Now does that sound like a chill to you?"

Parker Harland dropped the doctor's sleeve as if his hand was suddenly unable to keep a grip. His mouth tried to work, but no sound came out.

Doc Franklin reached over and clasped his friend's shoulder. "Let me go deliver this baby, then I'll come back and see how she's holding." He shambled down the stairs and down the sidewalk. As he passed Bethan, his frosty green eyes focused upon her. He gave a single nod, patted her head and said, "You're a good friend, young Miss Keane. And your mother is an angel in disguise. Tell her I said so." Then he was gone.

Bethan forced leadened legs to carry her up the steps. She stopped in front of Jodie's father and tried to think of something to say. But no words came. There was the sound of the gate opening; she glanced at two neighbors coming up the walk. She turned and entered the house. Maybe an adult would be able to find words for the stricken man.

Bethan passed through the downstairs, calling Jodie's name as she entered each room. Then she spotted her friend at the top of the stairs. Jodie was scrunched up smaller than Bethan thought possible. Knees up to her chin, her arms wrapped about her stiffly, she was holding her legs and her body in a tight ball. Her eyes remained fastened on the closed door to her parents' bedroom.

Softly Bethan climbed the stairs, eased herself down, waited a long moment, then reached over and put one arm around Jodie's shoulders. Sounds drifted up from downstairs, deeper voices and adult-sounding words, but it was as though they came from another world.

"They won't let me go in to her," Jodie finally whispered. "I don't understand. I was the one who got her into bed. Why can't I be with her now? What if she needs me?"

Bethan did not know what to say, so she said nothing. She just sat there, holding her friend, sharing her heartache.

There was a long silence between them, then Jodie turned to face her friend. In a voice soft but filled with anguish, she said, "I don't remember how to pray."

"Of course you do," Bethan replied softly.

Jodie gave her head a tiny shake, barely a shiver. "I've tried and I've tried. But I can't find any words inside me."

Bethan reached out her other hand, took both of Jodie's. They felt like ice. "Then I'll say the words for you," she whispered.

CHAPTER FIVE

JODIE'S WORLD BECAME ANCHORED on Bethan, the only reality that kept her from flying apart in a million tiny pieces. She knew her friend would be there just after dawn, and stay with her through each day of endless sameness.

Jodie was not allowed in the sickroom, which was an agony beyond belief. She followed the course of the illness through Doc Franklin's terse reports. She came to know two more new words, but this time she would have given her very life itself never to have heard them.

Bulbar poliomyelitis.

When the afternoon sun slanted around to the back of the house, Jodie and Bethan climbed onto the second-story gable, settled themselves into the angle of the roof, and gazed in through the white veil curtains. The soft light bathed her mother's bed and turned the waxed oak floor into a golden pond, upon which Louise drifted in and out of dreams. With each passing day her eyes seemed to grow larger. And darker. As though pain and sorrow were pooling in her gaze, along with her helplessness and her awareness of what was soon to come.

Louise seldom spoke. Her breathing was harsh and

labored. Whenever she was awake and alert, she would turn her head and simply lie there, watching her daughter. It hurt Jodie's heart to hear her mother struggle to breathe. But she would not leave her perch until the sun's shadows lengthened, and her mother's wan face was no longer visible. Bethan stayed with her throughout each long vigil, silent and still.

Her father, distraught, had never felt so helpless. "All my life I've spent mixing potions and helping people," he repeated over and over to each new visitor, often more than once. "Then what happens, my own wife gets ill and I can't do a thing for her. Not a thing! I feel like my whole life has been a waste!"

By the third day, Doc Franklin no longer had the heart to keep Parker away from his wife. Instead, he quarantined off the upstairs. Moira set up a camp bed for Jodie downstairs in the back parlor and came over twice a day to take a tray to the top of the steps, then return to stand over Jodie and make sure she ate her own food.

The evening of the ninth day Jodie did not come down from her perch at all. In the way of country folk, the neighbors also knew it was time, and gathered outside on the front lawn. The pastor was among them. Jodie sat on the gabled porch eaves, not aware she was holding Bethan's hand, much less squeezing it so hard the fingertips were turning blue. She watched through the curtains as Doc Franklin entered the sickroom and set the lantern down by the bedside. Jodie looked at her mother lying there. It truly was her mother, though her face was changed beyond all recognition. Illness had reshaped her mother in just nine short days. No, not short. Jodie felt that the rest of her life would not be as long as those nine days.

Doc Franklin fed Louise another spoonful of medi-

JANETTE OKE & T. DAVIS BUNN

cine, then took her pulse. He listened to her chest, then straightened with a long, low sigh. Parker watched his movements in numbed silence.

"The Lord be with you, Louise Harland," the doctor said quietly and shuffled from the room.

Louise accepted a drink from her husband, then turned toward the open window. In a hoarse whisper, she called, "Jodie?"

It took the girl a moment to find her own voice. "I'm here, Momma."

"You are my heart's delight," her mother said, the laboring breath making every word an effort. "My love will always be with you. Always."

Jodie forced her voice to make the words. "I love you too, Momma."

Her mother was silent for a long while. When she spoke again, her voice was clearer and calmer than it had been in days. "I'm tired now, Parker. I have to sleep."

The matter-of-fact tone broke him to pieces. "Don't go, Louise. I beg you."

"I must." Simple, direct, clear. "It is time."

———— ✿ ————

Harmony's undertaker was Mr. Timmons, a tiny figure of a man who scarcely weighed as much as his somber black suit. His house was situated next to the rectory, which was convenient; with a minimum of fuss people could file from the funeral home to the church to the cemetery. The Timmons' place was double-fronted, one door opening to where the family lived, the other to the hall where the deceased was laid out for the final gathering. Bethan sat there now, her hand holding Jodie's, and remembered all the times they had joked over how it would be to live next door to a funeral parlor. As she sat and watched the townsfolk pass by the sealed coffin, she reflected that she would never be able to look at this home and smile and joke again.

People filed solemnly by, stopping first by the coffin, touching the edge, looking down, many offering a simple prayer. The women held handkerchiefs crumpled to their trembling mouths. The men carried hats up close to their hearts, faces uncomfortable with the task at hand. Even those who saw Parker Harland every day were reduced to fumbling formality when they stopped before the grief-stricken man and offered him their hands. Some he took, clinging to them with abject brokenness. Others he did not see because of his unchecked tears.

They moved on. Another halt, this time in front of Jodie.

She stared at the coffin, even when the view was blocked by people stopping in front of her. The hand Bethan held was as cold and blank and lifeless as Jodie's eyes. Many of the women bent down to hug her and whisper a few words into her ear. Jodie neither responded nor looked their way.

Later the two girls walked the short distance to the church together, and it seemed to Bethan that all the town was there to stand and do homage to Louise Harland. No one seemed to think it odd that Bethan was there with the grieving family throughout, leading Jodie up the endless aisle and into the front pew, one hand still holding hers, the other arm now wrapped about her shoulders to offer both strength and guidance. For it was clear to all who looked their way that Jodie was going nowhere this day on her own.

Afterward they left the church and waited as the pallbearers brought out the coffin. Together the silent procession walked the short distance to Louise Harland's final resting place. Bethan's brother, Dylan, walked strong and straight, the coffin's front right handle upon his shoulder, setting the pace for the other pallbearers, though it was hard to imagine how he could see to place one foot in front of the other for the tears. Parker Harland made it down the lane and through the gates and up to the open grave site between the pair of great oaks only because he had a strong man on either side, hands gripping his shoulders and keeping him upright.

Jodie's gaze remained upon her mother's coffin, blind to everyone and everything about her. Bethan guided Jodie forward, willing her own life and warmth into her friend. As together they passed between the cemetery's stone gates, Bethan thought it was uncommonly strange how even the normally joyous church bells could toll the day's sorrow, how even the overcast sky could draw a veil across the sun's sweet springtime brightness, as though the whole world were pausing in its steady turning to bid a soft farewell to a fine country woman.

CHAPTER SIX

THE AFTERNOON AIR felt so thick and heavy with heat that Bethan imagined it tasted salty to her tongue. Maybe it was the perspiration that moistened her skin which made her think of salt. She wasn't sure. Nor did she really care. It was too hot to even think straight.

She glanced over to where Jodie sat rocking silently beside her. Almost three months had passed since her mother had died, and still Jodie spoke scarcely a word. Sorrow blanketed her as heavily as the heat. Bethan was left with a feeling of helplessness and frustration that she could not do something for her beloved friend.

The porch swing squeaked as it rocked back and forth. Bethan listened to the protest of its worn hinges, to the hum of the honey bees in the bougainvillea. Nearby, a pair of hummingbirds disputed the rights to the hollyhocks, darting back and forth to challenge each other, neither gaining much from the sweet nectar.

Bethan brushed dampened hair back from her forehead. "Would you like to—"

Jodie shook her head before Bethan could complete the question.

"Go see Sherman?" Bethan persisted.

Again Jodie indicated no.

There was silence as the swing squeaked on. "Would you like some cold lemonade?" Bethan finally ventured.

Jodie looked about to decline one more time, then nodded her assent.

"Do you want to come to the kitchen, or shall I bring it out here?"

"Here," was the terse reply.

Lemonade seemed like a trivial thing at such a time of grief and longing, but Bethan was glad for something to do and for the response from Jodie. She hurried in and was soon back with two tall glasses, their sides already frosted from the cold contents. The hummingbirds chose that moment to call a truce and share the hollyhocks, though they stayed some distance apart, each feeding from opposite ends of the patch.

"Did you know hummingbirds are very . . . very territorial?" Bethan observed, glad she could use the word and hoping to engage Jodie in *something*.

Jodie nodded.

"I've seen them have some real scraps," Bethan went on. "It seems so strange. They are such little creatures, and so beautiful, you'd expect them to be sweeter—nicer to each other."

Jodie stirred restlessly. For the first time her eyes came to life, but not with her usual interest in the world. Rather, the eyes flashed with angry bitterness. "Things are often different than they seem."

Bethan glanced uncertainly at her friend over the edge of her lemonade glass.

"The preacher is always saying that if you are good, God will take care of you. Isn't that so?"

Bethan gave a hesitant nod. Those were not the exact words she remembered, but maybe something like that had been stated. And at least Jodie was talking again.

"Well, it's not true," Jodie went on. "Momma was good all her life."

"I know she was," Bethan quietly agreed, understanding where the dark thoughts were headed.

"So why did—" Jodie's emotions made her voice tremble, but she began again. "Why did she have to leave me?"

Bethan set aside her glass of lemonade and reached a hand out to Jodie. "You miss her very much, don't you?" she said, her own voice full of emotion.

Jodie did not even bother nodding her agreement.

"Momma was talking about it the other day," Bethan continued. "She said your mother was one of the finest women she had ever known. She said it's hard to understand why someone like her had to go so early."

Bethan stopped and sought more of her mother's words. She couldn't remember them exactly. Nor was she quite sure they were the words Jodie needed to hear. But she didn't know what else to say to her friend. "Momma said that maybe God saw she was ready for heaven and her reward. That her mission on earth was done. That—"

"Her mission!" Jodie's eyes were flashing again. "What was her mission?"

Bethan was taken aback. "I . . . I don't know. Maybe being . . . being kind to people—"

"She was my *momma*," Jodie cut in with vehemence. "Don't you think that was a mission? Being my momma?"

"Of course it was." The words seemed so weak, so flimsy. But she could think of nothing else to say.

"She wasn't done with *that*." The words were flung angrily at Bethan.

Instinctively Bethan set aside her mother's words.

They had sounded good and comforting when spoken to her, but she knew in her heart they were not what Jodie needed to hear. They would not bring comfort and healing to her friend, lonely and in deep inner pain from the loss. Bethan's eyes filled, and her chin quivered as she sought the words of her own heart.

"Jodie, I don't know, I don't understand why your momma died. But I know if it had been my own momma—" And the impact of that thought, the *reality* of it as she sat there beside her friend and fully shared the loss for the first time, caused the tears to run freely down her cheeks. Her words were barely a whisper as she forced them through trembling lips, "If it were Momma, I'd feel so awfully sad. I'd be so lonesome. I think I'd just cry all the time."

Before Bethan could speak another word, Jodie leaned her head against the smaller girl and began to weep. Bethan placed her arms about her friend's shoulders, and they cried together. The squeaking hinge, the sultry day, even the dueling hummingbirds were completely forgotten in their moment of shared grief.

———— ❧ ————

"Momma, are we poor?"

"The questions you ask." Moira was too busy with her dinner preparations to look around. "We are doing quite well, thank you kindly. Who put such a thought in your head?"

Bethan pulled silverware from the pocket in her apron and polished it before setting it down. Late afternoon sunlight streamed through the big window behind her, warm and welcoming. It was the last week in October, seven months since Louise Harland's funeral, and though the first frost had not arrived, the days were becoming both shorter and cooler. "Oh, just something I heard the teachers talk about at school today."

"Well, they most certainly were not talking about us," Moira harrumphed as she dusted the counter-top with flour, lifted the wet towel off the big mixing bowl, and brought out the biscuit dough. "We do not have much but, thank the good Lord, we have enough, and a bit left over."

Bethan nodded her agreement and continued setting the big hardwood table. Their kitchen opened directly into the dining area, forming Bethan's favorite rooms in the house. They held all the fragrances of Moira's cooking and were lit by a great bay window which looked out over Gavin's vegetable garden and the fields beyond. The rectangular table Gavin had made with his own hands, his first gift to his new bride. The afternoon light caused the beeswax-polished wood to gleam with a ruddy glow.

Bethan's mind went back to the conversation she had heard in the hallway after school. She had waited until all the students had left to make her departure. That week the doctor had pronounced that her eye was not improving, and the only thing to do was for her to wear the eyepatch every day for two months. Bethan had been horrified, but the doctor had been insistent, repeating his solemn warning that the lazy eye might otherwise go blind. Her mother had then included her own voice with the doctor's, and that was that. Bethan hated the eyepatch almost as much as she hated the way the others picked on her. So she arrived at school early and slipped through the halls alone unless Jodie was around. After school she waited until all the other voices disappeared into the distance before venturing out.

As Bethan had walked down the lonely hallway, she had stopped at the sound of the two voices up ahead. It had been an argument, really, between Miss Charles and the teacher Bethan was most frightened by, Mrs. Sloane. She shared the same large frame as her daughter, Kirsten, and had a way of tightening down her face that made even the wildest of children quiet down in fear.

Mrs. Sloane's voice held a quiet fury that had backed Bethan around the corner and out of sight. "You're doing nothing but building up the hopes of these poor village children so they can be destroyed."

"I most certainly am not the one intent on destruction," Miss Charles replied, her voice tight. "Jodie Harland has every right to compete."

Jodie. They were arguing over her best friend. Bethan moved up to the side wall and edged as close to the corner as she dared.

"She will disgrace herself and this school," Mrs. Sloane lashed back. "Children from those big-city schools will make her look backward and us foolish for even considering putting her in the competition."

"Well, we should let her have the chance to change an ill-conceived perception," Miss Charles responded. "She absolutely amazed the judges at the town spelling bee, not to mention winning here in our own school. One of the town judges even said she was a shoo-in for the state finals."

"I have been teaching these children far longer than you have been on this earth," Mrs. Sloane snapped. "If my experience has taught me anything, it is that poor village children are not up to this sort of challenge. And I most certainly discount anything a local judge says about one of our own. As should you, if not for your sake, then for the sake of this poor child."

"And I am telling you that Jodie Harland is one of the most brilliant young ladies it has ever been my pleasure to teach," Miss Charles replied, her voice shaking with anger. "As to the challenge, we shall never know for certain, will we, since you are refusing me the chance to use the school's discretionary funds."

"Absolutely out of the question. Such a thought is simply absurd. The family is not destitute. If this were such a good idea, the father could certainly afford to pay for his own daughter to travel to Raleigh."

"We went all through this in the administration meeting. Parker Harland has been simply devastated by his wife's death. He can scarcely remember his own name, much less see to the needs of his daughter." Miss Charles' voice took on a desperate note. "I beseech you, think of what this might mean to the child."

"That is exactly what I am doing," Mrs. Sloane replied, her tone full of cold satisfaction. "I am guarding this child from a disappointment which might crush her fragile spirit."

"But—"

"This matter is closed. Good day, Miss Charles." Heavy footsteps echoed behind her as she stalked down the hall.

———— 🌿 ————

"Bethan!" She wheeled about at the sound of her mother's voice. "Child, you have been staring out that window for nigh on ten minutes. What on earth has gotten into you?"

"Nothing, Momma." Hastily Bethan returned to setting the table.

"I declare, sometimes I think you lack the sense God gave a baby bird." Moira shook her head as she slid the biscuit tray into the big cast-iron oven. She straightened, raised the edge of her apron, and wiped at the perspiration on her forehead. "I do wish a bit more of Jodie's common sense would rub off on you, considering how much time you spend together."

Bethan put down the last of the cutlery, turned, and said quietly, "I heard them quarreling, Momma."

"Quarreling? Who, daughter, who? I need me a noun."

"The teachers. After school. They were arguing about her."

"About Jodie?" Moira dropped her apron. "As if the child didn't have enough to worry about already, living in that house with a shadow for a father and a memory for a mother." She inspected her daughter's face. "It was bad, was it?"

Bethan nodded worriedly. "I think so."

Moira sighed and walked over, reaching out to embrace her daughter. "Bethan, Bethan, child, you are too precious for this earth, and that is the plain and simple truth. You have a heart of pure gold, and more love in you than I ever thought possible for one sparrow of a child to hold." She stroked her daughter's hair, murmuring, "How ever will you find your way in this world?"

Bethan returned the embrace, her head filled with the fragrances of her mother and the meal she was preparing. "I'll be all right, Momma. The Lord will take care of me."

"I do so hope and pray you are right." Her mother eased herself down into a chair and smiled sadly. "Soon after you were born, I had the strangest thought come to me. I was looking down at your little face, and already you had the most winning way about you. Eyes so clear you could see heaven in them, and a smile that would break your heart. I thought then that perhaps you were one of the Lord's precious angels who had wandered down and been born by mistake."

Bethan looked at her mother, saw the sadness mingled with the love. "Why do you worry about me so much?"

"Perhaps I shouldn't," Moira agreed quietly. "But I can't help myself. I see the love shining in your little face, and I remember . . ."

"Remember what?"

It was a while before Moira answered. Her voice was low when she finally said, "I recollect just how hard life can be." A shadow passed over her features as she said the words. "My dad, your grandfather, may the blessed Jesus watch over him, was a miner. As were my three elder brothers."

Bethan nodded. This much she had heard, but little else. She only knew her mother's parents from the gilt frame on Moira's dressing table. The couple stood in front of a white slat house badly in need of fresh paint. The man wore a dark suit and string tie in the manner of one unaccustomed to such finery; the sleeves hung crooked, his coat was open to reveal suspenders, and his collar rode up his neck where one collar stud was missing. He wore a narrow-brim hat from the last century, a walrus moustache, and an expression which suggested he rarely if ever smiled. His wife stood beside him, dressed in a simple neck-to-ankle black frock. Her hair was fastened back tightly, her mouth finished in deep downward-sloping lines, and her eyes looked very, very tired. Bethan's mother always referred to them as the hardest-working folks who ever lived, but had said little else of her life before coming to America. Until now.

"We lived a miner's life," Moira went on quietly, "in a village climbing the side of a Welsh mountain, one road in and one road out, all the houses on our little lane owned by the same pit that employed the four men of my family. I was very young, but I remember, child. Oh yes, much as I would like to forget, the memories are etched deep upon my mind and heart."

Bethan stood and looked into her mother's eyes, saw the dark gaze turn inward. One hand continued to stroke Bethan's hair, but she doubted her mother even knew what she was doing. Moira's accent became more pronounced as she continued, "I remember well, with a child's clarity and a child's pain. I remember how the coal dust settled on everything, turning even the rain a sodden gray. I remember how my father's hands would never clean up completely, no matter how hard he scrubbed. Nor his face, with the wrinkles deeper than they should have been for a man his age, all darkened like veins in the earth with dust from the mine. I remember dear sweet Harry, my eldest brother, and how he coughed his life away. I remember how we stood at the graveside, my poor mother weeping as though it were her own life that lay in the coffin with her eldest son, and how my father swore then and there we would find a place to live where the sky was blue and the air was clean and the life was worth living."

"And so you came here," Bethan said quietly.

"Aye, that we did." Moira's gaze refocused upon her daughter. And a smile formed, one which was so full of love that it made Bethan's own heart ache. "And I met your darling of a father, and had this angel of a daughter, whose face shines with the light of heaven, and who worries me to distraction with her addled ways."

"I don't know who's the addled one," Dylan announced, his heavy boots treading into the kitchen as the screen door slammed behind him. "But I sure do smell something that's near about overdone."

"My biscuits!" Moira leapt up and raced for the stove. She used her apron to open the door, fanned away the smoke, pulled out the pan, and pronounced, "And not a moment too soon." She turned about with, "I'll thank you to go clean yourself up, sir. You look as though you've brought half the pigsty in with you."

"You're welcome," Dylan said with a deep bow, offering Bethan a wink and a glimpse of his easy grin, then ambling out.

Moira's gaze followed her son from the kitchen. "How that boy can manage to smile, with him barely a year from conscription, is a mystery I shall never unravel. Not in all my days."

Bethan felt the same chill every time mention was made of the war in Europe, the one people were already calling The Great War. Most of the time it seemed so distant from Harmony—the papers occasionally predicting how the United States was bound to become involved was about as close as the conflict came. That and the difficulty in buying things like fuel oil and rubber parts. Otherwise, the war might as well have been on the moon as far as their town was concerned. "But Dylan's only just seventeen," Bethan heard herself protest. "The war can't go on so long that he'd be taken."

"Your words in God's ears," Moira sighed, lifting a lid and stirring the contents. "Now come over here and help me, daughter. Reach up and get me the big serving bowl—yes, that's the one. And tell me what it is you heard the teachers say about Jodie."

————— 🌿 —————

After a discussion that continued all through dinner, Bethan was sent to find Jodie and deliver the news. It being Wednesday and Wednesday being market day, the Harland Apothecary was still open to serve outlying farmers. Jodie was there behind the counter with her father, as she was almost every afternoon and all Saturday. She was very matter-of-fact about her work, as she was about much of her life since her mother was gone. The apothecary was the only place, she told Bethan, where her father showed much interest in life or spoke more than a few words. It was nice to be able to talk with him, even if it was only about his business. Plus she loved the work and the smells, she went on, and besides, anyplace was better than the hollowness of their home.

When Bethan pushed through the double screen doors, Jodie was busy with a farm woman whom Bethan did not know. She could hear Mr. Harland moving around in the back room where ingredients were mixed and packaged. Bethan hung back, inspecting row after row of unfamiliar items. She was suddenly very shy about her errand. It was hard of late to anticipate Jodie's reaction to anything. She had become so reserved since her mother's passage, so self-contained. Even Bethan was confused at times about just exactly where Jodie's mind might be.

"Well, I just don't know, Miss Harland," the heavyset woman was saying. "My family's been using blackberry balsam against colic ever since I was a child."

"And you were just telling me it wasn't working on your youngest." Jodie showed an amazing amount of patience when working. She stood calmly, apparently willing to meet every objection reasonably but head on. "That's why I thought you might like to try this new seltzer compound. Many of our customers have been pleased with the results."

Bethan sidled on down the aisle, listening with one ear as she inspected the display of bottles and boxes. Her admiration for Jodie and her remarkable intelligence increased every time she stepped into the apothecary with its supplies. There on the shelf stood Dr. Worden's Female Pills—for weak women, sallow complexion, and absence of strong blood. Then came Dr. Hammond's Nerve and Brain Pills, followed by Dr. Rose's Arsenic Complexion, the glass bottles wrapped in delicate white tissue. Boxes of Reliable Worm Syrup were stacked alongside the Twenty Minute Cold Cure and Laxative. She picked up a box of Electric Liniment to better see the label—a fist holding lightning bolts. The last rows were for the Egyptian Pile Cure, bottles of Vin Vitae Wine of Life, and White Ribbon Secret Liquor Cure.

"But it's sixty-seven cents," the woman complained. The lacquered black cherries on her flat hat shook with indignation. "I could buy three bottles of the blackberry balsam for that price and have change left over besides."

"If one bottle didn't work, it's unlikely three would do any better," Jodie pointed out. She leaned across the counter. "Why don't you try it this once, and if it doesn't work, bring back what's left and we'll refund that part of the price."

"Oh, very well." The woman opened her shoulder bag and brought out a battered coin purse. "I don't mind telling you, that young'un has been worrying me something fierce. Seems like he's been in pain and colicky far too much this autumn."

Jodie wrapped the box in brown paper, tied it with

twine, accepted the coins, and handed over the package with a smile and a query. "What are you feeding him?"

"Only the best. We've had ourselves a right good late crop of greens, what with the warm weather and all."

"Turnips are known to cause gas in some children," Jodie pointed out. "You might want to cut them out for a week or so, and see if that helps."

The woman cocked her head in thought about the young lady's comment. At length she nodded, making the cherries bob again. "Well, thank you. I'll surely do just that." The woman gathered up her purchase, lowered her voice, and asked, "How's your daddy keeping?"

Jodie's smile became a little forced, in Bethan's view. "Just fine, thank you. Doing just fine."

"Well, you're a help and comfort, I am sure, helping out like you do." The woman patted Jodie's hand. "Bless you, child."

When the woman had trundled out the front door, Bethan walked over and quipped, "Listen to you, giving out advice like a doctor."

"It used to scare me something awful, these people asking me all sorts of questions," Jodie admitted. "Some of the things that come up you wouldn't believe."

"I don't even want to hear," Bethan said.

"I told Doc Franklin about it. He said these country folk don't like calling out the doctor unless life or death is hanging in the balance. He stops by every day or so, picks up his supplies, and lets me ask him anything I like." Jodie shook her head, her expression full of wonder. "He says he's just helping to prepare his replacement."

"You'd make a good one," Bethan said, though the thought of a woman doctor startled her.

"I told him I didn't want to become a doctor," Jodie said, "but he doesn't listen when I talk like that. Doc

Franklin says his hearing is becoming mighty selective in his old age."

But Bethan did not want to speak about her best friend's desires for the future. Whether a doctor or a scientist, such discussions always became linked to Jodie going away somewhere else, a thought that Bethan could not abide. "Can we talk?"

"Sure."

"What about your father?"

Jodie did not even glance around. "Daddy lives in his own little world when he's in the back."

Again there was that disconcerting matter-of-factness. Bethan was unsure what to say. Jodie seemed to be growing into someone else, someone she did not really know. Bethan hesitated, then said quietly, "I heard Miss Charles talk about the state spelling bee."

"Oh. The championships this spring." Jodie's calm maturity failed her, and she became once again the young girl Bethan knew. Her shoulders slumped as she sighed, "She spoke to me too. I can't go. I was hoping that something would happen. But Daddy, he won't even talk to me about it. He's not budging out of town, and he doesn't like the idea of me going off alone." She seemed to struggle for a moment, as if trying to present an unconcerned face to the news. But it slipped away. "I don't care," she said sadly.

"Yes you do. And you should." Bethan allowed a glimmer of her own excitement to show through. "Because you're going to win."

Jodie gaped at her. "What on earth has gotten into you? Didn't you hear what I just said?"

Bethan nodded happily. "It's all arranged. Momma's going to talk with Miss Charles tomorrow morning. She and Daddy are going to be your official—something, oh, now I can't remember the word."

"Chaperons," Jodie said softly, her eyes growing round.

"That's right. Chaperons. And here's the best part. We're all going up together. Me too. On the *train*. To *Raleigh*."

"You're not just joshing me," Jodie said, her voice scarcely above a whisper. "Not about this."

Bethan saw the light growing in Jodie's eyes and suddenly could scarcely keep from dancing in place. "There's more. We'll have to miss two days of school. And we're going to stay in a *hotel*. And we'll eat in restaurants, with waiters and *everything*."

Jodie whirled around the counter, grabbing up both of Bethan's hands. "You mean it? You really mean it?"

Bethan stared into her best friend's eyes and saw there the first real joy in what seemed like years. A joy so fierce it hurt Bethan's heart to look at it. You deserve this, she wanted to say. You, more than anybody. But she didn't want to cloud the moment with any mention of what Jodie had been through. So all she did was return the grand smile and say, "Really."

CHAPTER SEVEN

THE WAR CROWDED in the instant they boarded the train for Raleigh. Up to that point, Jodie and Bethan had paid it no more mind than they did the fight for universal suffrage. They were too young to be affected by either, and there were other pressing matters which required their immediate attention. They left it to the old men who gathered by the Harmony courthouse and around the benches outside the apothecary to talk about both issues. Usually it was an argument as to which would destroy them first, a president who had gotten them involved in Europe's war, or giving women the right to vote. Most felt the latter to be far more dangerous.

The train ride from Harmony to Raleigh brought the war up close—too close for comfort, in fact. The cars were crowded with khaki-clad young men hardened by basic training at Fort Bragg, clutching precious travel passes as they went home a final time before being sent overseas. Their packs cluttered the passageways. The air was thick with their loud chatter and smoke from their cigarettes. Younger boys hung over the backs of their seats, innocent eyes bright with envy and the excitement of distant battles. The soldiers, some of whom seemed barely older than the kids who competed for their attention, reveled in the chance to play heroes.

Jodie and Bethan sat crammed up against a window. Moira and Gavin tried to present a stern front to the nearest soldiers, but the boys were paying it no mind. One of the most handsome of the group leaned across the back of their seat, looked straight at Bethan, and said, "I'd be obliged, miss, if you'd favor me with your address, so's I can write once I'm settled."

Bethan blushed a deep rich scarlet. In her best Sunday outfit, with her hair brushed until it shimmered a rich copper-gold, and the hated eyepatch left in Harmony, she fulfilled Jodie's early prediction of being the prettiest girl in the county.

Moira answered for her daughter. "I'll be thanking you to mind your manners, young man," she snapped, her voice lilting with indignation. "My daughter happens to be barely on nodding terms with her fifteenth year."

"Momma," Bethan protested mildly, her color even deeper.

"Yes, ma'am, I can surely see that," the young fellow responded, touching his cap to Moira, as unabashed as ever. "That's why I'm gonna be writing on the outside of this here note that she can't open 'til she turns eighteen." He turned sparkling green eyes back to Bethan. "You see, missie, soon as we've done gone and won us this here war, I'm gonna be coming by and asking you to marry me. That's what my letter's gonna be saying."

Bethan could not take him seriously. Especially when she saw the twinkle in his green eyes.

But Moira's indignation turned to anger. "That's more than enough of that," she cried, brandishing her folded-up Chinese lacquered fan. "You'll be turning around and minding your own affairs and leaving us in peace!"

"Yes, ma'am," the handsome young soldier drawled. Ignoring the laughter and comments from his fellows, he kept a friendly eye fastened upon Bethan. "Just as soon as that pretty thing gives me a kiss to seal the bargain."

Bethan raised both hands to hide her face and giggles. But his bold statement proved too much for Moira. She rose in her seat and whacked at the soldier with her fan. To the cheers of his fellow soldiers up and down the coach, the young man raised arms in protection over his head and slid back down into his seat.

Moira harrumphed herself back down, her face red with exertion. She looked across the aisle to where her husband sat and huffed, "A fat lot of help you were."

"Oh, Moira," Gavin said shakily, wiping his eyes with the back of his hand. "I wish you could have seen yourself, I truly do."

"Well, somebody had to defend our daughter's honor, and it surely wasn't you." She snapped open her fan in disgust, and the poor thing gave up the ghost, showering Moira's lap with shreds of bamboo and colored paper. She looked back at her husband. "Just look what you've gone and done now."

This was the final straw. Mirth spilled out of Jodie in great waves of laughter, as though all the months of grayness were being pushed away in a single moment of release. Gavin sat beside his daughter, his solid girth bouncing in glee, while Bethan covered her face with both hands and tried to smother her giggles. Moira looked askance from one to the other, until she too gave into the moment, and laughed out loud. She raised the poor battered fan and made a parody of trying to fan herself, sending further shreds in every direction. The soldiers to either side joined in the laughter, then crowded close, demanding to know who they were, where they were going, and what for.

News that Jodie was traveling to compete in the state spelling bee resulted in pandemonium. Before she knew it, strong arms had her up and steadied on top of a seat and against the compartment wall. From the position where everyone could see her, with every face turned her way, voices throughout the coach began shouting out words for her to spell.

On and on the words kept coming. Her face flaming with some embarrassment and even more excitement, Jodie spelled out the answers. As the words became more and more difficult and her answers continued to be correct, the coach gradually quietened.

Finally there was only one who kept calling out words, a dark-suited gentleman near the far wall, resplendent in a pearl-colored silk waistcoat and mutton-chop sideburns. His voice resonated throughout the now-silent car as he called, "Leprechaun."

Jodie spelled it swiftly.

"Pneumonia."

"Obfuscate."

"Illiterate."

"Conundrum."

After that word, there was a long pause as the man studied her. Then he simply said, "Remarkable."

Jodie started to spell it as well but stopped as the entire compartment began cheering, and she realized that he had meant the word as a compliment. The soldiers whistled and clapped their hands and shouted as the man walked over and extended his hand. "I am Dr. Walton Connolley," he said when the noise died down. "And you are a most astounding young woman. What is your name?"

Jodie blushed and slid back down into her seat before introducing herself.

"Do you have any plans for your future, Miss Harland?"

"I want to be a scientist," Jodie said, her voice quiet but firm.

Dr. Connolley's face did not mirror the surprise shown by Gavin and Moira Keane at this announcement. Instead, he studied her for a moment, then gave a single brief nod. "I am Chancellor of the State College in Raleigh. When you have completed your schooling, I suggest you write to me. We shall see then what further can be done." He tipped his hat to the group. "Now I shall bid you good day."

The four of them remained in astonished silence as Dr. Connolley walked back and resumed his seat. Gavin finally breathed, "Well if that don't beat all, I don't know what does."

The handsome face appeared above the seat, and the young man announced to Bethan, "You're still the one who's won my heart, missie. Say you'll stay truly mine 'til we're back home again."

"That will do, young man!" Moira's voice rang out, to the repeated mirth of all the surrounding soldiers. "And this time it won't be a fan I'll be applying to your head."

Jodie joined in the laughter, watched her friend blush once more with pleasure, and decided this trip was already the best thing that had happened to her in a long, long while.

Bethan had never seen anything like Raleigh. And the more she saw of the city, the less she was certain if she liked it.

For one thing, the war was everywhere. Uncle Sam pointed at her from every wall, every mailbox. He looked big and strong and accusing, demanding that she give up her precious brother to a war she did not understand. Not at all. For once she agreed with the irascible old men who gathered on the courthouse steps back home and wished they had never even heard of all those countries over in Europe.

Ribbons and bunting were strung throughout the city's main streets, for Raleigh had recently had its own enlistment and war bond parade. Bethan could not abide the thought of celebrating the war, so she imagined as hard as she could that all the red, white, and blue banners were really there to celebrate Jodie's arrival.

Her friend could scarcely have been happier. They checked into the Hotel Sir Walter, a great bastion of stone and big windows right in the heart of downtown. While Bethan was still sitting on the edge of the bed and trying it out for bounce, reveling in the fact that she and her friend were to share one whole room to themselves while her parents slept next door, Jodie was already impatient to return downstairs to the lobby.

When they were settled in chairs by the side wall in the ornate reception area, Jodie watched the world with wide-eyed fascination. After the longest while, she breathed, "Isn't this grand?"

Bethan looked around the lobby, wondering if she was missing something. To be honest, she was becoming somewhat bored. She searched for something positive to say and settled on, "It surely is big."

"Not the room," Jodie said. "*Everything*. The people, see how they come parading through here as though they owned the whole world? And look over there, the waiter serving those people tea; I bet it's real silver, that pot. And look at the stole that woman has around her neck, and here it is, warm as anything. And look out front, that man climbing out of that automobile; he's got himself a driver opening the door for him. Have you ever seen the like?" Her words tumbled over each other in her excitement.

"No, never," Bethan answered quietly.

With a sudden flash of understanding, Bethan knew Jodie was leaving. That someday, somehow, Jodie was going to make her home somewhere other than Harmony. That Jodie would leave Harmony with the ease and the eagerness that she might cast aside an uncomfortable corset. That Bethan was going to lose her best friend.

"Everything is so different here," Jodie said, as though confirming Bethan's thoughts. "It's all so gray at home these days. I don't mean the color gray. How it feels. Daddy hardly ever speaks once he's done with work. He walks around sighing or humming these little tunes I don't think he even hears. He'll sit for hours with a journal in his lap, not turning the page."

"It's been so hard for you," Bethan said softly. "And you've been so brave." But her thoughts remained fastened upon the realization. Everything which defined Bethan's world, everything she loved besides this brilliant flame of a young lady, would never be enough to hold Jodie. It did not matter that Jodie's departure was going to be long in coming. That it was to come at all was almost more than her poor heart could stand.

"What's the matter?" Jodie demanded, peering at her. "You've gone all white."

"It's nothing, really," Bethan said, rising to her feet. "Maybe just a little tired out from the trip. I'll go see if Momma and Daddy are ready for dinner."

CHAPTER EIGHT

THE NEXT MORNING Bethan found Jodie downstairs sitting in the same overstuffed horsehair chair. "There you are. What time did you get up?"

"I don't know. Early. I didn't sleep very well—the spelling bee and all." Her eyes inspected Bethan's outfit. "Is that new?"

"Yes." She wore a Gibson girl dress and a straw hat with a blue ribbon. She lifted the hem and asked shyly, "Do you like it?"

Jodie smiled her approval. "It's beautiful."

"Momma bought one, too. She says it's the first new dress she's bought herself in she didn't know how long, and while she was out, she might as well . . ." Bethan's voice trailed off as she watched her friend's face crumple. "What's the matter?"

"Nothing. It's . . ." Jodie stopped, then said through a trembly little smile, "It's beautiful, Bethan. Really."

"I've said something wrong, haven't I?" Bethan felt the brightness fade from the day. "I'm always doing that."

"Don't talk nonsense. You do nothing of the sort. You're the kindest, sweetest person I've ever met."

"Then why did you get so sad all of a sudden?"

"I was just thinking . . ." Jodie had to stop a moment. "Of my momma."

"Oh, Jodie." Bethan reached out her hand. "And just listen to me chatter on." She turned to briskness. "Well, we've got plenty of time for a nice breakfast, and then we can go back up to the room and have a little prayer together before we go to the meeting hall."

"Thank you, but I'm not hungry," was Jodie's response.

"Well, at least come and sit with me. Then we can go back upstairs and ask God to be with us through the day." Bethan smiled in anticipation. "And for His help for you in the spelling bee."

Jodie's gaze turned blank. "Thank you for the invitation," she said calmly. "But I don't wish to pray."

Bethan's voice mirrored her confusion. "What on earth do you mean?"

"I would appreciate it if you never speak to me about religion ever again." Jodie said the words with frankness and determination.

Bethan could not hide the shocked look that washed over her face. "What?"

"You heard me. It's something I do not ever care to discuss again."

The tears sprang to Bethan's eyes, as though the shock had to have some way of expressing itself immediately. "But what are you saying?"

"I am saying exactly what I mean."

"But I see you in church, every Sunday you're there—"

"With my father," Jodie finished for her. "Daddy needs me. I don't want to cause him any more trouble than he's already got. But I'm not sure God even exists, and if He does, then I don't want to have any part of Him."

Bethan's mouth opened and closed, but the words did not come. Finally she whispered, "You don't mean that."

"Oh, but I do." The calm iciness of Jodie's voice was more brutal and frightening than any rage. "As far as I am concerned, no God worth worshiping would ever have taken away my mother."

Bethan reached for her friend. "But, Jodie——"

"You heard me," she said, sitting upright and calm in her chair. "Not ever again."

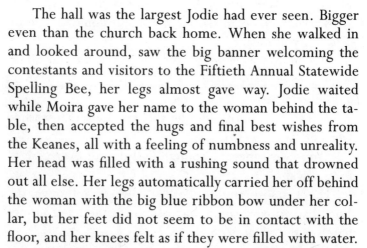

The hall was the largest Jodie had ever seen. Bigger even than the church back home. When she walked in and looked around, saw the big banner welcoming the contestants and visitors to the Fiftieth Annual Statewide Spelling Bee, her legs almost gave way. Jodie waited while Moira gave her name to the woman behind the table, then accepted the hugs and final best wishes from the Keanes, all with a feeling of numbness and unreality. Her head was filled with a rushing sound that drowned out all else. Her legs automatically carried her off behind the woman with the big blue ribbon bow under her collar, but her feet did not seem to be in contact with the floor, and her knees felt as if they were filled with water.

"My, but aren't you calm," the woman said cheerfully. "If I were the youngest contestant—fifteen, isn't it?—why, I'd be near about ready to faint."

Unable to find her voice, Jodie made do with a nod. That was exactly how she felt.

But the woman laughed gaily as she led Jodie up the

stairs, across the stage, and behind the big velvet curtains. "You, now, you look perfectly at ease. How on earth do you do it?"

Jodie managed a shrug and looked around the gathering. It was easy to see that the other contestants were older and more mature—but it was also true that some of them looked very nervous. She guessed there must be fifty or sixty people, all under the watchful gaze of three stern-faced chaperons. Every eye turned her way for a moment, and Jodie felt her heart quake.

The woman patted her shoulder. "I'll just leave you in these good people's capable hands. Good luck, my dear."

"Phenomenon."

"Tobacco."

"Medieval."

The words began on what Miss Charles would have called an intermediate level. Jodie was relieved to find that others shared her nerves, because even at this stage contestants were being dismissed right and left. If one person misspelled, the word then went to the next. Her first two words came in this way, which granted her the advantage of more time to think them over. Even so, she felt as though her mind were scattered in a thousand pieces, and spelling the simplest of words was the hardest task she had ever faced.

"Rhinoceros."

"Irascible."

"Auspicious."

The hall was huge and filled to overflowing. Each time

a participant was dismissed, they were sent off with polite applause. Otherwise the crowd was tense and watchful and silent. The voices of the referee and the contestants bounced back and forth over the great open space. Jodie's voice sounded high and frail to her own ears.

"Connoisseur."

"Supercilious."

"Quixotic."

The words grew increasingly difficult. As the number on stage dwindled, the applause grew louder for each departing contestant. Jodie's heart felt as though it could not beat any harder. When it came time for her to spell "incandescence," her voice quavered so that she was unsure the judges could make out what letters she was saying.

Then the whole scene before her altered.

The change did not come gradually. Not at all. In one great blanket of calm, a gentle peace descended upon her. She felt her surroundings come into focus. She became shielded against the pressure and the tension under invisible wings of love and comfort and serenity.

"Plenipotentiary."

"Concupiscence."

The contestants were dismissed one by one. Only four were left. The applause was thunderous now, each correct spelling bringing cheers. Yet the tension which brought a sheen of perspiration even to the judges' foreheads did not touch her. The referee called out, "Apocrypha." Jodie spelled it silently to herself, as she had most of the words throughout the contest. The older contestant standing beside her hesitated, then said, "A-p-o-c-r-i-p-h-a." When the girl had been applauded off the stage, Jodie spelled it, her voice now clear and bell-like. She was rewarded with a great cheer from the crowd.

Without warning, Jodie had the sense of a realization flooding her mind. The thought was so sudden and so striking that she momentarily lost awareness of everything about her. *This peace is a gift from God.*

The thought had the force of a mirror placed before her heart. She could not escape the conviction that though she had turned away from God, still He was there, waiting for an opportunity to return to her, and return her to Him.

Jodie had a sudden flash of memory, not of an experience but rather of an emotion. Once again she felt the pain of her mother's passage, and yet this time overlaid was the gentle sense of the Lord's presence, offering her hope and healing. But her reaction was immediate. With a strength that sent a shudder through her entire frame, she shook off the invitation and the threat of again feeling all those emotions she had strived so hard to put behind her—the loneliness and the hurt and the sense of abandonment.

All this, from the sudden realization to its rejection, took less time than a half-dozen heartbeats. The hall and the contest returned instantly into focus, but the gift of peace was gone. Jodie looked around the audience, and in a sudden flood felt all her fears come crashing back.

The referee turned to her and intoned, "Bougainvillea."

Jodie began spelling, but there was such an echo throughout the great hall, and she felt a sense of overwhelming tension. She reached the final "l" and suddenly could not remember if she had already said one or two. She hesitated a long moment, then added one more.

A rippling sigh ran through the crowd. The head judge called out, "Jodene Harland is dismissed."

It was over.

She stood there stunned. She wanted to shout out that she knew the word, that she had been confused by the echo. But before she could speak, the applause rose and broke over her, wave after wave of great cheers. She glanced at the other contestants, realized there were only two left besides her. The cheering continued. But it did not raise her up. Instead, it felt as though all the crowd and all the noise was battering at her, pushing her around and urging her back and off the stage.

———— ✥ ————

Jodie clutched the tall silver statue and the fifty dollar war bond, her prizes for coming in third place. She could see the Keanes struggling to approach through the crowd clustered around her. Everyone wanted to get a closer look at the youngest finalist ever in a state spelling bee, clap her on the back, chatter words that Jodie scarcely heard. Two photographers flashed bright lights in her face before moving off. She felt as though her smile were plastered into place.

Finally the Keanes were able to get close enough to hug her and shower her with more excited words. Jodie endured it all, trying hard to play the part of a tired but happy contestant. She allowed them to lead her from the hall, feeling eyes upon her the entire way.

She waited until they were outside and Bethan's parents were a few steps ahead of them to look at Bethan and quietly ask, "Were you praying for me in there?"

Bethan gave her a surprised glance. "Of course I was."

Jodie walked on in silence. Her confusion and resistance created an internal storm.

Bethan gave her a desperate look. "Don't ask me to stop," she pleaded, misunderstanding her friend. "I couldn't do that. Not ever. I pray for you every night and every morning. I thank God for making you my friend. I pray that He will heal your heart." She examined Jodie's face, then added, "And now that I know how you feel, I'll pray that He finds a way to bring you back to Him."

Bethan walked alongside Jodie, her gray eyes wide and anxious. When Jodie did not say anything, she begged, "Don't ask me to stop. I couldn't, I just couldn't. It'd be easier to stop breathing."

———————— ✿ ————————

Bethan hummed as she scurried about the dining room, checking to see that everything was in perfect readiness. She wasn't sure if it was happiness or nerves that brought the song to her mind. She decided the table could use a bit more polishing, and her thoughts made tight little circles along with the cloth. What if no one came? What if the whole thing was a flop? What if Jodie didn't show up?

"Land sakes, child. Isn't that the third time you've been over that table?"

Bethan watched her mother enter the room, the punch bowl sloshing gently with lemonade. "I want everything to be just right."

"And well you should. But you'll be wearing the shine off, not putting it on." Moira settled the bowl down on the table and began placing cups and saucers around it. That done, she settled a white linen cloth over the lot to hide it from view. "You're sure she doesn't know? Jodie's far from slow witted."

101

"No, she isn't, but I don't think she knows." Bethan began setting little sandwiches on the crystal platter, one her mother had polished until it shimmered. She walked over and placed it under the cloth as well. "We haven't even mentioned her birthday."

Moira hurried out to check the two pies baking in the oven. The chocolate layer cake—Jodie's favorite—was already prepared and set in the dining room. "What ruse did you settle on to bring her over?" she asked as Bethan followed her into the kitchen.

Bethan had to swallow. Even with her mother agreeing, it had been hard to even hint at a falsehood. "I said I needed help with my choir piece."

"Which is true enough, far as it goes." One by one Moira drew out the blackberry pies, tested them with a knife, and carried them into the dining room. They needed to set a moment before they could be cut. The rooms were instantly filled with the fragrance of fresh fruits and cinnamon. She returned to the kitchen and said, "She should be in the church choir herself, and that's a fact."

Bethan nodded agreement. It had remained a bitter disappointment that Jodie refused to join her in the church choir. It turned out that Jodie had inherited her mother's pleasant voice, and she was finally persuaded to join the school choir, much to her mother's delight. Earlier on, Bethan had dreamed of the two of them singing duets together before the congregation. But when the time finally came, Jodie turned her down flatly, not even listening to her arguments about how a voice as fine as Jodie's should be used in lifting praises to God. "She won't even talk about it," Bethan disclosed. "There isn't anything I can do to change her mind, except pray and hope for a miracle."

A knock on the back door drew their attention. Bethan nervously cast a glance toward the front parlor, wondering if Jodie would choose this moment to appear. Two girls stood on the stoop, holding wrapped gifts in their hands. Bethan greeted them warmly and beckoned them inside. "Is she here yet?" one asked excitedly as she passed Bethan her shawl.

"I told her seven. I wanted to be sure everyone was here first."

"She doesn't suspect anything?"

"I don't think so."

Both girls looked pleased. Surprises were so delicious.

Swiftly the kitchen and parlor filled with excited chatter. Bethan kept one eye nervously upon the clock as she admitted one friend after another, hoping they would all arrive before Jodie showed up.

The idea for a surprise birthday party had first come to Bethan a week before. The two girls shared almost everything, including their age. For part of the year the number was the same for both girls. And then last week Bethan had referred to Jodie as being fifteen, the same age as herself. "Sixteen," Jodie had corrected. With shock and a pang in her heart, Bethan realized she had forgotten Jodie's birthday. "Sixteen," Jodie had repeated. "I turned sixteen last Tuesday."

The matter-of-fact yet empty way she had spoken the words stayed with Bethan all through the day. Jodie had had a birthday, and not one person had paid it any mind. In tears she had discussed it with her mother that night. "She never mentioned it, and I forgot. I suppose her father did too."

Moira had been incensed. "Well, we certainly needn't allow it to happen again. We'll be asking her to supper ourselves. If that noodlehead of a father can't care for his own, we'll just have to see to things here."

The idea of a simple family dinner had evolved into a full-blown surprise affair to be held the following week. Bethan had grown so excited over it all that she had scarcely slept a wink. It wouldn't matter that it would be a bit later than the actual day.

Finally the last of the guests arrived. Bethan looked around the circle of school friends. Everyone had come.

She waved to catch the attention of the chattering girls. With a nod toward the mantel clock, she addressed them. "She'll be coming any minute now. Stay in here and be quiet. She always comes to the kitchen door. I'll bring her in here to the piano. As soon as I draw up the shades, you all jump up and shout 'Happy Birthday.'"

An excited twitter passed through the room, followed by a chorus of shushes. Bethan hurried back to the kitchen, feeling her heart pounding with excitement and nervousness. She paced as she waited for the rap at the door. Jodie was always punctual.

At one minute before seven, Bethan heard steps on the back porch. She wiped damp hands on her skirt and moved to the door. She reminded herself that she needed to try to remain casual through the first few minutes.

She opened the door almost before Jodie had finished the first knock. For once she was thankful for the porch's dim lighting, which might help to hide her strained smile. "On time as always. Come on in."

Jodie entered and took off her summer hat, setting it on the kitchen table. She sniffed the air. "Has your momma been baking again?"

Bethan had not even thought about the aromas. She forced a laugh. "You know Momma. She's always baking something."

Jodie nodded. "So where's the music that has you puzzled?"

Bethan took a deep breath and steered her toward the front parlor. "In here. I left it on the piano. I've been trying to pick my way through it, but you know me. My . . . my music reading skills aren't nearly as polished as yours." She rushed through the explanation and kept up the determined chatter as she led the way across the hall. She gently ushered Jodie in before her, stepping aside and leaving her best friend standing alone at the door of the room. Which was exactly how Jodie was when the shades swept up and an enthusiastic chorus of "Happy Birthday" filled the air.

Jodie's head jerked upright. For one moment she looked utterly confused and bewildered.

As their friends gathered around, chattering and laughing gaily at the effect of their surprise, Jodie turned to Bethan. Her eyes said far more than Jodie, with all her gift for words, had ever spoken. In that instant Bethan knew that her busy week of planning and thinking had been well worth the effort. This was one birthday Jodie Harland would never forget.

CHAPTER NINE

"I'M NOT SURE."

The words were barely a whisper. Bethan tipped her head slightly and studied herself in the gilt-edged oval mirror by her bureau. Her hair was piled in a strange heap of curls at the top of her head, with a large black-and-white ribbon tied precariously on one side. It made her feel as though it would all come tumbling down if she moved too quickly.

"I think it is positively beautiful," Jodie announced.

It was hard to question Jodie when she was this certain about something. "Don't you think it's a little, well, strange?" Bethan dared ask.

"I think it is stunning." Jodie patted at a wayward curl. "Not to mention extremely daring. It's just like that 'do' I showed you in the magazine, the one at the apothecary. They say it's all the rage in New York."

"I'm not sure I want to look daring," Bethan confessed and shook her head. Immediately she realized her error. The heap of curls threatened to spill over her ear.

"Don't," cried Jodie. "You'll have it all coming down and we don't have time to fix it again."

Bethan watched her reflection as Jodie adjusted a

couple of the pins to hold her locks in place. Doubt still plagued her. She didn't look stunning. She looked silly. "I don't think I want to go to a picnic looking like this."

"Sure you do. Just think what the boys will say."

The idea brought Bethan's head up sharply, pulling a silken curl from Jodie's fingers. Jodie responded by giving Bethan an impatient little thump on her shoulder. "Stop wiggling. I'll never get it right if you keep jerking about."

The upsweep looked anything but right as it was. "I've never seen anyone wear their hair like this," Bethan protested.

"That's the whole point. We want to be daring. Adventurous. The boys will never notice us if we look just the same as all the other girls."

Bethan wasn't sure she wanted to stand out this much. "How are you going to do your hair? There isn't time before the picnic to pin it up."

Jodie poked the last pin solidly into place, then reached into her pocket and drew out a page torn from a magazine. "Like this."

Bethan tipped the page so the window's light fell across it and gasped. "She has *cropped* hair."

"Isn't it chic!" Jodie enthused. She reached into her pocket and withdrew a pair of barber's scissors. "Now let me sit down and let's start."

Bethan recoiled in horror. "Your beautiful long hair—Jodie, you can't be serious."

"Oh, hush up and hurry." Jodie settled herself before the mirror, examined herself critically, and with both hands measured out a length that would scarcely cover her ears. "I think that would be about right, don't you?"

Frantically Bethan sought a way out. "What will your father say?"

Jodie shrugged and brought the measuring fingers up

JANETTE OKE & T. DAVIS BUNN

half an inch shorter. "He won't even notice. He never notices anything about me."

"Oh, Jodie," she sighed. It had to be so difficult, living with a father who did not seem to know his daughter was even there. Jodie's simple words melted Bethan's heart. But not her resistance. "I can't. I just can't. Look, if we're not downstairs soon we'll be late."

"How can you be late for a picnic?" Jodie was not giving up that easily. "They last most of the day."

Bethan cast a nervous glance at the scissors. "Momma won't think she's on time unless she's the first woman to place her baskets on the table."

To her intense relief she heard an impatient tread at the bottom of the stairs, followed by Moira's voice calling up, "Are you girls planning to go to the picnic today or next week?"

"Just a moment, Momma," Bethan sang back, casting an I-told-you-so look at Jodie.

"If I stood around and waited for you, we'd never get out of the house," Moira snapped back. "I am now commencing to count to ten."

Jodie jumped from the vanity stool, knowing as well as Bethan the folly of attempting to cross Moira. It cheered Bethan greatly to see that she left the scissors on the bureau.

The two girls descended the stairs and entered the kitchen. "Can we carry something, Momma?" Bethan offered.

"Your father has already loaded . . ." Moira caught sight of Bethan, and her voice trailed off.

Bethan froze in midstep. She had forgotten about her hair. She had a breathless sense of waiting for a sharp rebuke but, instead, Moira's nose began to bother her something terrible. So bad, in fact, that she had to turn away with her handkerchief and wipe it with both hands. When she finally turned back, her face was still pinched, and her voice shook slightly as she said, "You two go out and get yourselves loaded up."

Bethan's father was standing by the side door of their new automobile, watching Dylan as he settled the last basket into the space behind the seat. "Sure you don't mind taking the horse and meeting us there?" Gavin did not wait for a reply but turned to greet the girls. And saw Bethan. He gaped for a single moment, then swept out his own checked handkerchief and was seized by a paroxysm of coughing. Bethan was about to go over and help with a few whacks on his back but was afraid her hair would fall down if she did.

"Something must have . . . must have gone down wrong," Gavin wheezed, wiping his eyes. "You look awful pretty, Jodie," he said, turning to Bethan's friend.

"Thank you." She smiled and raised the hem of her dress in a curtsy. "Mrs. Keane bought it for me."

"I know she did and I'm glad of it. Parker didn't raise any fuss over it, did he?"

The crisp, matter-of-fact tone returned. "I doubt he even noticed."

Bethan glanced at her friend, her heart aching as it always did when Jodie spoke that way. Moira had taken both girls shopping the week before, after several passionate discussions with Gavin when they no doubt thought Bethan was out of earshot. But Bethan had listened carefully to them talk about how Jodie was filling out her dresses to the point that they looked like they were going to burst. It wasn't right nor proper, Moira had repeated several times, how that father of hers did not even use the eyes God gave him to realize his daughter was growing up and needed new clothes.

Dylan chose that moment to clamber out of the black Ford's narrow confines. He straightened up, caught sight of his sister, and his jaw dropped to his chest. But before he could say a word, Gaviñ turned him bodily in the general direction of the stables. "Don't just hang about there; saddle up old Jessie or you'll be late."

"I was just going," Dylan said, his eyes fastened on Bethan as he walked straight into the gatepost. Recovering, he threw one further glance back toward his sister and hustled away.

Bethan gave her friend a very hard look. Maybe the New York style wasn't such a grand idea for a Harmony picnic after all. Jodie avoided Bethan's gaze by giving the distant woods a very thoughtful inspection.

"What are you all standing around like that for?" Moira clumped down the stairs and walked around the automobile. "We'll positively be the last ones arriving." She opened the Ford's door. "Get into that rumble seat, girls. And, Gavin, I want you to drive just as fast as you possibly can. You know how I dislike being late."

They all hurried to obey. Mr. Keane adjusted the control knobs before moving to the front of the automobile. When he began cranking, Jodie leaned over to watch with wide, excited eyes.

The engine coughed to a start, then sputtered. Gavin pushed his hat back before leaning over to crank again. Moira rapped the steering column with her parasol as she often did when the Ford was misbehaving. This time, the engine took hold with a hearty roar. Mr. Keane ran for the driver's side and flung himself into the seat.

They chugged off down the street, stirring up the dust and making the dogs howl in excitement. Bethan could not recall ever having driven this fast before. The wind clutched at her hair with impatient fingers. When Jodie closed her eyes to the cool breeze, Bethan helped things along by giving her hair a good shake. A second shake, and all the tresses came tumbling down. "Oh," she cried over the engine and the breeze. "Look what happened."

Jodie opened her eyes to see Bethan's entire face covered by half-pinned clumps of hair. The two girls stared at each other for a moment, then began to laugh. Moira turned in her seat and gave a satisfied nod as the girls, shaking with mirth, struggled to find all the wayward hairpins.

It was a glorious spring day, not yet burdened by the heaviness of humid summer heat. Children romped about the field with the energy of young colts turned out to pasture. Newly greened shrubbery sparkled with a freshness that the countryside dust had not yet tarnished.

"I've been so looking forward to this," Jodie said calmly, once the girls had helped set out the picnic hamper and were free to wander. "I haven't been out anywhere in, oh, it seems like years."

Bethan hated it when Jodie talked like this, the emotions all carefully stored away. She tried to engage her with, "Look, there's Annabell Clemens, and all the Morrells. It seems like the whole school's here for the church picnic."

Jodie's gaze fastened on a group of boys and some of the fathers tossing a ball back and forth. "Let's go watch them play."

Moira called out after them, "Mind you both remember your good upbringings. I won't have any child of mine acting like a common floozy."

"Yes, Momma," Bethan returned and hastened to catch up with Jodie. "Do you understand about football?"

Jodie shook her head. "No, but we'll catch on. Just holler when the others do."

The game swiftly turned into a tightly fought match. Many gathered to watch and cheer on the two teams.

Bethan wasn't sure how she felt about football. Even this friendly match between families she had known all her life looked more like a war than a game. Nobody on the field was smiling anymore. And everybody kept shouting things. There was a great deal of bumping and falling and pushing and smacking.

"Which team is ours?" she finally asked.

Jodie pointed across the field. "The ones over there. They've got the cutest boys."

At that moment, one of the tall, strapping lads came rushing over to grab the ball, surprising them so that they shrieked in unison. He paused long enough to flash them both a wide smile before running back on the field. The suddenness of it all left Bethan breathless. She and Jodie shared a wide-eyed look, then turned back to watch the game with new interest. Bethan started to ask if Jodie wasn't glad she had not cut her hair, but decided to stay quiet on that one. There was no reason to bring a cloud into this beautiful sunny day.

———— ✿ ————

Bethan sat in the empty church, not wanting the quiet moment to end. Not just yet. She watched the dust motes dance in the afternoon sunlight streaming through the tall side windows and felt so incredibly fortunate. A strange thing to be thinking, she knew, when she lay awake for hours each night worrying. But it was true. Finally she sighed and released the moment by rising to her feet. As she walked down the silent aisle, she felt yet again how blessed she was to have Jesus to turn to when times were bad.

She pushed through the church doors and spotted Jodie

seated on the bench across the street. She walked over and sat down. A giant magnolia spread sweet-scented shade above the two girls, fresh as the spring in white dresses.

Jodie watched a great gleaming car purr by. To have something to say, Bethan asked, "What kind was that?"

"A Packard."

"I never can get all the different kinds straight in my head."

Some people would have thought it strange, how Jodie knew every make and model of automobile on the road. Bethan knew it was not the cars which attracted her but rather the freedom they represented. Bethan hesitated a moment, then asked because her heart would not let her keep still, "Do you think maybe tomorrow you might come in with me and pray for—"

"I thought you understood. I really don't want to talk about it," Jodie said, her voice calm yet utterly firm. "Not ever again."

Bethan nodded sorrowful acquiescence. Almost a year had passed since their journey to Raleigh, and still the only time Jodie ever set foot in church was when her father felt up to going. If he was having one of his "bad spells," Jodie would still dress up on Sunday mornings, then simply walk the streets until it was time to come home. She refused to discuss her feelings, refused to even let the subject be broached.

And yet for the three weeks since Dylan had received his call-up notice, Jodie had accompanied Bethan each afternoon to the church and waited outside while she went in to pray for her brother's safety. Jodie had been there and held Bethan when she had cried herself empty the day Dylan had left, listened to her choked voice pray that God would keep her brother safe and bring him back with his smile intact. Jodie had sat there and patted Bethan's shoulder and seen her through, as she had every day since then.

Bethan sat beside her best friend and sent another silent prayer lofting upward that the Lord would find a way to open Jodie's heart to Him again. And do it soon.

"The newspapers are growing more positive every day," Jodie told her. "A delegation has been sent to Berlin and was received by the Kaiser's representatives."

"Really?"

Jodie nodded. "There was an article this morning that predicted the Armistice would be signed before long."

Bethan's heart soared. She did not understand exactly what Jodie was saying, but she knew her friend read the papers as hungrily as she did almost every book within reach. "So they might be sending Dylan home?"

Jodie smiled, and that simple gesture was a remarkable symbol of her flourishing maturity. "I would imagine there will be a lot of work to be done once the war is over. But at least he will be saved from having to face combat."

"Oh, thank God," Bethan breathed, clasping her hands together.

Jodie rose to her feet. "I have to be going."

"Back to the apothecary?"

"No, Miss Charles asked me to come by this afternoon. Want to walk with me back to school?"

"Sure." With any other student, such a summons would have been cause for anguish. But with Jodie so far ahead of everyone else in the school, the teacher's request had to mean something different.

They stopped to pick flowers for their hair. It was a daily habit now, and had been for weeks, ever since Jodie had read about it in the *Saturday Evening Post* magazine. She had shown it to Bethan, a color drawing of a beautiful Parisian lady, out for a stroll on a busy tree-lined street. And the caption read, "The perfect accompaniment to a lovely lady's wardrobe—the freshness of a springtime blossom in her locks." Jodie had stared at it so hard and so long that Bethan wondered if perhaps her friend was seeing something that she did not.

There was no need to take flowers from gardens. Harmony's streets were lined with blossoms and flowering trees. Veils of honeysuckle were traded for tulip poplar blossoms, and they for dogwood. Brilliant purple flowers from crepe myrtle trees seemed to make Jodie's eyes darker than they already were. Sprigs of cherry blooms were Bethan's favorite, with their fragrance so light it appeared almost shy, as though her own spirit had found a home in something as beautiful as this flower.

Jodie pulled off a magnolia blossom as big as a pie plate. When she put it in her hair the hand-size petals covered her face from forehead to chin, and they laughed so hard they had to sit down. Bethan loved to watch Jodie laugh, and to laugh with her. It did not happen very often anymore, not even in the games of imagination Jodie made up herself. Jodie rose to her feet once more and danced from tree to tree, pulling blooms off in frantic haste, tossing one away to make room for the next, as though one of them might prove to hold some magic strong enough to turn her wishes to reality and fly her off to a fancy Paris street. A place where lovely ladies wore long flowing dresses with tight waists and colorful scarves over their powdered shoulders, and flowers were bought from smiling old women in flower stalls, rather than picked from trees, just like Jodie read about in the magazine.

Bethan shivered when Jodie talked like that, trying to push such dreams away, and with them the fear that her friend would truly fly away. Bethan never wanted to live anywhere but Harmony. In truth, she did not much care for these fantasies of Jodie's, with their visions of being somewhere else, of travel and adventure and a life of accomplishment. But she could never refuse her friend such games. The yearning and the hunger in Jodie's heart was so strong it burned like fire in her eyes. No, Bethan loved this unusual young woman far too much to refuse her a chance to dream her dreams with another, even if they did hurt and frighten her so. When Bethan caught sight of that determined flame burnishing Jodie's dark gaze, or heard the brilliant intelligence of her thoughts, she wondered if Jodie had in truth ever really been a child at all.

The flowers in Bethan's hair were in sharp contrast with her sober thoughts as she slowly made her way home after saying goodbye to Jodie at the school.

———— ✀ ————

Jodie entered the school building with a sense of dread. She was fairly certain she knew why Miss Charles wanted to see her, and it was the last news in the world she wanted to hear. The very last.

The evening before when she had been making a delivery for her father, she had seen Miss Charles coming out of the train station. She had returned home, her heart a hollow gourd. If Miss Charles left Harmony, there would be one less person with whom she could really talk. But Miss Charles was going to leave. Why would she stay? She did not have family here. There was nothing tying her down. She could go anywhere she liked. Jodie knew if she were Miss Charles, she would be on the next train out. But the very thought of Miss Charles going had left Jodie with legs encased in lead, her feet dragging sadly in the dust.

Jodie now walked down the silent hall, stopped in front of her classroom, and knocked on the closed door.

When a muffled voice answered, she opened it and said, "Miss Charles?"

"Oh, good, it's you. Come in."

She entered the classroom and glanced around. It was empty save for them.

Miss Charles rose from her desk with a bright smile of welcome. She wore an appealing dress of pink and white, and with her coppery hair and touch of rouge on her cheeks, she looked like one of the Parisian ladies in the magazine. A happy one. "Go sit down in that chair next to my desk. I will be right back." She left, closing the door after her.

Jodie walked over and seated herself. The air smelled of chalk and heat. The silence seemed strange, as though uncomfortable after the noise and energy of the now-departed students. Through the open window came the sound of children filled with spring fever.

"My goodness, these are heavier than I thought." Miss Charles came into the room, her arms wrapped around a wooden crate. She shouldered the door closed, walked over, and put down her package. She looked at Jodie, her eyes dancing with excitement. "I have a surprise for you."

Jodie gaped at the teacher. "For me?"

Miss Charles nodded and reached for the scissors. She began cutting away the binder twine. "One of my closest friends from school is now assistant librarian at State College. I had her send these to me. They arrived by train yesterday evening."

That explained why she had seen Miss Charles at the railway station. Jodie felt a great burden lift from her shoulders. Miss Charles wasn't leaving after all. "What is it?"

"Something to occupy you this summer. You have just one year left here, and I assume you still want to go to college."

Jodie nodded slowly. "But my daddy is against it. He says I should stay here and take over the shop. He says I don't need college to do that."

Miss Charles stopped and asked gravely, "Has he forbidden it?"

"No. He wouldn't do that. At least, I don't think he would." Jodie hesitated. "Daddy doesn't have the strength these days to be that definite about anything," she said candidly. "He's just told me he doesn't like the idea and won't help me with the cost."

"Well, I suppose we should be thankful for small blessings," Miss Charles said. She pulled open the top and pulled out a very large book. She handed it to Jodie with a smile. "Besides feeding that voracious mental appetite of yours, we will now need to prepare you for the scholarship panel."

The book weighed heavily on her lap. Jodie read the title aloud, " 'Introduction to the Natural Sciences.' " She looked up at Miss Charles. "You did this for me?"

"Jodie, I am going to treat you as an adult and speak with you plainly." Miss Charles seated herself, reached over, and took one of Jodie's hands. "You have a remarkable mind. More than that. You have a gift for learning. Call me selfish, if you will. But I want to be a part of this, to help you find your wings and begin your soaring flight."

Jodie looked down at the book in her lap, but the cover was now so blurred she could not read the words. She whispered, "Thank you, Miss Charles."

Politely taking no notice of Jodie's emotion, she rose to her feet and began taking the books out one by one. "There also are some very fine novels here—oh, good, she remembered to send the book on biology as well. I imagine that might slow down even you for a while."

Jodie sat and watched the pile of books beside her grow ever higher. She felt suspended in space, unable to take in what was actually happening.

"I would suggest that we meet once a week and discuss whatever you wish." Miss Charles smiled down at her. "I cannot promise that I shall be able to answer your questions, or even keep up with you once you really get started. But if I cannot give you the answer myself, I promise that I will try and find someone who can. Is that all right?"

Jodie had to make do with a nod, unable to grasp the concept of having a question that Miss Charles might not be able to answer.

"And you must feel free to ask me anything that comes to mind. Anything at all." The teacher sobered momentarily. "But I think it would be wise if we kept our discussions to ourselves, Jodie. You must tell your father, of course. But no one else. I must always be seen as impartial within the classroom, showing no favorites."

Jodie started to agree, then hesitated. "Can I please tell Bethan? She won't tell anyone. She's my very best friend."

CHAPTER TEN

CHASED BY A BLUSTERY December wind, Jodie hurried back from school. It was remarkable how the weather had changed so suddenly. Only the week before it had seemed as though Indian Summer would remain with them until Christmas. This morning, however, dark winter clouds had cast a sullen blanket over the sky, and the wind had turned bitter. She stepped into the apothecary and blew upon her hands. Then she heard the discussion.

"You have a gift of a daughter. A prize. A miracle." Moira Keane's peppery spirit spilled forth in the words. "She is destined for great things. All the teachers are talking of her." A hesitation. "Do you even hear what I am saying to you?"

"I hear you." Jodie's father's voice was gruff. "All the world is hearing you."

"Then hear this as well, Parker Harland." Moira's lilting accent became more pronounced with her emotion. "Your daughter is growing into a beautiful and intelligent young lady, and you are missing out on it all. It is time you let the past go and see what wondrous miracles God is making in your life and hers right here, right now. Let

Him restore you, and grow beyond your pain."

When her father did not reply, Jodie peeked around the corner far enough to watch. Parker remained frozen in stillness for a very long while, seemingly captured by Moira's gaze and the power of her words. Then he shrugged, one tired and defeated gesture. He dropped his head and turned and walked into the back room.

Moira sighed as well, mirroring the man's defeat, and began sliding her wrapped packages into her carry bag. Swiftly Jodie backed up and left the apothecary. She understood her father and his reaction all too well. It hurt too much to bring up what they both in their own way kept bottled inside.

The apothecary door opened and shut behind Jodie. "Oh, there you are." Moira stepped up to her, tucking wayward strands back beneath her scarf. "You mustn't remain out here in this wind, dear. Especially with the flu still creeping about. You'll catch your death."

"I was just going in, Mrs. Keane."

Moira took her arm and led her back inside. She glanced to where Parker had disappeared into the back room, then turned back to Jodie and lowered her voice. "Your dad has left you to founder, hasn't he?"

Jodie pretended not to understand. "What do you mean?"

Moira's gesture paid her words no mind. "If ever you need an older woman to speak with, dear, you just remember me."

For some reason Jodie suddenly found her chest burning something fierce. She swallowed the lump in her throat and managed, "Thank you, Mrs. Keane."

"You're quite the young woman now." She gave Jodie a sad smile. "Hard knocks have a way of making a body grow up fast, don't they?"

Jodie nodded solemnly. "Faster than I'd ever wish on anybody."

Moira reached around and hugged Jodie with her free arm. "Ah, child, child. You are one in a million, you are. I thank my lucky stars for whatever blessing brought you into my darling Bethan's life, and that is the truth as clear as I know how to say it." She loosened her grasp and looked at Jodie with genuine fondness. "I know it's hard for you to accept my words just now, but I believe with all my heart you're going to turn out fine."

Jodie searched the older woman's face, then said quietly, "I'd like to believe you."

"Trust me you most certainly can," Moira agreed confidently. "I don't know that you have chosen an easy road through life. But I do know in my heart of hearts that you have what is required to make good at what you seek to do. Long as you remember to turn all that is and all that happens over to the Lord's care, and count on Him in your loneliest hour."

Jodie felt the coldness creep into her soul. "I'd rather not talk about that, please."

"Bethan had mentioned this to me. It sorrowed me so I did not wish to believe her, even though my daughter couldn't lie her way out of a dark corner." Moira fastened Jodie with a knowing gaze. "Listen to me, my strong-headed young lass. My own beginnings were hard. I won't say harder than yours, though I might. A heart that knows sorrow loses the ability to compare. I will just tell you that I have walked a road marked and rutted as your own. I too had every reason to grow bitter. I could have turned my back on the Lord above. But I chose to trust Him. I cannot say that I understand His ways, but this trust has served me well. It has comforted me through the hard times, and blessed me with joy when there was goodness about—and with peace when there wasn't." She peered deep into the young girl's eyes, nodded once. "You just remember that."

Jodie made do with a nod.

"Well, enough of that, then." Moira's tone turned brisk. "I suppose Bethan has told you that Dylan is arriving home on this very afternoon's train."

Jodie had to smile. "Only about ten times an hour for the past two weeks."

"We'll be having a little celebration this evening to welcome him home. You're as much a family member as the rest of us, and besides, you look as though you could use a festive night yourself. Bethan was too busy preparing Dylan's favorite dishes to come, so she asked me to stop by while I was out doing errands. She wanted to make this dinner with her own two hands, though I'm not certain what kind of welcome that's going to make for the wayward lad." She stepped toward the door. "Seven o'clock sharpish, if you please."

Jodie was very grateful to be included in the Keanes' evening, and not just because Dylan was returning home. Her father was becoming more and more morose, stumbling about the home in a gray fog all his own, seldom speaking at all. Jodie fed him a light supper, standing over him to make sure he ate. The entire time he did not say a word, not even when she said she was going out for the evening.

Jodie slipped out of the house wrapped in her heavy coat and shawl, and still felt the wind's frigid fingers working their way through and under and around. It was always like this the first few days of winter. Harmony was so warm so much of the time, even in the heart of winter, that it was surprising just how cold certain days could become.

Bunting and banners still were everywhere in Harmony, though after a full five weeks of bands and speeches and welcoming parades, folks were gradually growing quieter, and life was returning to normal. It was no longer necessary to stop on every corner and say how wonderful it was that the Armistice had finally been signed, and the boys were coming home.

Jodie ran lightly up the front stairs to the Keane home and pulled the bell cord. When no one answered, she pushed open the door and let herself in.

Bethan came rushing up and grabbed her in a great hug, dancing her across the hall floor. "He's home! He's home! And wait 'til you see; he looks like a movie star in his uniform."

"You'd have thought we'd have all seen enough of war by now," Moira called from the kitchen. "But no, now that he's finally free of the service, Bethan insists he wear the uniform and remind us of how he was so long from kith and kin."

But tonight Bethan would not let her mother browbeat her into silence. She pulled Jodie into the parlor and called back to Moira, "You think he's as handsome as I do, now admit it."

"Handsome is as handsome does," Moira retorted from her post in the kitchen, but there was no sharpness to her voice. Not tonight. "I will admit that we have raised ourselves a dashing lad."

Heavy steps sounded on the stairs, and Gavin entered the parlor. He inspected the girls and said, "I'd have never imagined three ladies could make that much racket. I expect Dylan's going to think he's still back on the firing range."

Jodie smiled at Bethan's father. He had the kindest eyes she had ever seen in a man. "I haven't said a word, Mr. Keane."

"Of course you haven't. I said three only so you wouldn't feel left out. Bethan, for goodness' sake, let go of her long enough to take her scarf and coat."

"Well, well, would you just get a look at this."

Jodie spun about and was immediately shocked to stillness by the man who stood before her. Dylan was not the same youngster they had seen off only eleven months before. The face was more angular, the eyes keener, the back straighter, the body leaner. The result was the boyish Dylan now honed to a man's hardness.

Except the smile. He flashed that wonderful smile of his, the one which threatened to split his face and which lit up his eyes with the joy of it all. "This can't be little Jodie."

"Of course it is, silly." Bethan grasped her friend's inert hand and began swinging her arm in great excited sweeps. "Who on earth did you think it was?"

"I don't know for certain," Dylan replied as he approached and looked down at her from a height which Jodie did not recall ever noticing in Bethan's brother. "But this is a beautiful young lady, not the giggling youngster I left behind."

"I never giggled," Jodie replied, finding her voice at last. It sounded strange to her ears, low and breathless.

"Maybe it was my sister making all that noise by herself," Dylan conceded and held out his hands, becoming serious and gentlemanly. "May I take your coat, young lady?"

"Thank you." Jodie turned her back to him, and as

she did, she realized that all the eyes in the house were upon them. Even Moira had emerged from the kitchen to watch the exchange. Strange that she would not be smiling, especially since she had invited Jodie in the first place.

Jodie felt the coat lifted from her, then the shawl, each motion sending little shivers through her. He was close enough for her to capture a hint of his fresh smell, soap and something else, a spicy fragrance he must have used on his hair. She turned back to him, looked up, and wondered how Bethan's brother could have been transformed into such a handsome stranger.

Dylan's voice was both richer and hoarser as he said, "Yessir, you have grown up, Jodie. It makes me realize how long I've been gone. How old are you?"

"Almost eighteen."

Gavin laughed and said, "In about a year and six months, if I'm not mistaken. Or have you found some secret and pulled away from Bethan in age as well as school?"

Jodie blushed and dropped her gaze. The moment was suddenly swept away as Moira clapped her hands and said, "To the table everyone. This dinner won't be kept waiting a moment longer."

"Now that I've seen the army close up, I'm glad I missed the war. Real glad," Dylan said to his father. He paused long enough to shovel in the last of his butter-beans, then pushed his plate over to one side. He looked at Moira and declared, "That was one of the finest meals I've ever had in all my born days, Momma."

"You're thanking the wrong cook," Moira said, nodding in Bethan's direction.

Dylan's eyes showed surprise, then pleasure as he grinned at his sister. "Then Jodie here is not the only one who's been doing some growing. Thank you, Bethan." He reached over and squeezed her hand. As Bethan turned a bright crimson, Dylan turned back to his father and went on, "You ought to have seen the faces of the instructors, the ones who had done their time in the trenches. They looked like they'd glimpsed through the gates of hell itself."

"I wouldn't be talking like that around the town," Moira warned. "People might mistake you for a coward."

"Well now," Gavin said easily and waited while his wife subsided. "Coming from someone else, maybe. But from Dylan, why, I imagine they'll laugh and call it the voice of good sense."

Jodie nodded agreement. Most everyone around Harmony liked Dylan. His good nature was balanced with great strength and a rare willingness to pitch in whenever work needed doing. She glanced over at Bethan. She was listening to Dylan with rapt attention, hanging on to every word, her eyes scarcely leaving his face, her plate almost untouched.

Bethan now leaned forward and asked, "Well, if they weren't going to send you off to war, why did they have to keep you for so long?"

Dylan laughed, a great and easy sound. "The army kept me because it was easier than letting me go. I discovered the first week I was in that the army has a way of doing things that don't always make a lot of sense."

"But what did you *do?*"

"Most of the time I worked at one depot or another, repairing everything on wheels and some that weren't."

A flash of something more than easygoing humor appeared in his eyes. "Tanks, trucks, cars. Learned a lot about engines and the like."

"You must've enjoyed that," Gavin offered. "Never did know a boy who got as much pleasure out of taking things apart and putting them back together as you did."

"Sometimes not the right way," Bethan said with a laugh. "Momma, you remember the time he took apart your mantel clock, and when he put it back together he had a spring and a wheel left over?"

"The work suited me just fine," Dylan said to his father, unwilling to let this go just yet. "I always did like working with my hands, especially with machinery. The whole time I was there, I felt like I was getting ready for the future."

Jodie recalled the letters Bethan had received, with their postmarks from far-flung cities in Florida, Arkansas, Mississippi, even one from Texas. "You must have seen a lot," she said with longing in her voice.

Dylan turned, his dark gray gaze reaching across the table to her. He nodded. "Saw a bit of the world while I was out there, had myself some good times. Found out I love travel and adventure. If I can, I'd like to keep that a part of my life from now on."

Jodie suddenly discovered her heart had grown so full she could not draw a steady breath. Her voice was very small as she replied, "So would I."

Moira shifted in her chair and hurried to put in, "I'm not so sure the future holds anything much that I can look forward to. Seems to me, changes are being pushed on everything and everybody, whether we want them or not."

"I think the future is exciting and full of promise," Dylan said, releasing Jodie's gaze slowly. He turned to his mother and went on, "I love the challenge—the rush of new events."

"Too many new events, too much change," Moira replied. "The world is moving far too fast for my liking."

"Not for mine," Dylan answered. "It could never do that for me. This is going to be a world of machines, and I want to be a part of it."

"Sure seeing signs of that on near about every farm," Gavin agreed. "Folks are either learning new ways or worrying about being left behind."

"There, you see?" Moira looked from husband to son. "Just as I was saying."

Dylan announced to the table, "I've decided to open up an automobile and farm machinery garage. With gasoline pumps and repair stations and new motor cars and tractors for sale."

Gavin stared, then exclaimed, "Here? In Harmony?"

"Already talked to the Ford people about it. That's why I didn't come home three weeks ago when you were first expecting me. Used my military pass and traveled on up to Detroit."

"Detroit!" Jodie breathed, not paying any mind to the sudden looks from Bethan and her mother. "That must have been something."

"Sure was," he said, pausing long enough to flash her a smile. Then back to his father, "Turns out they've been looking for somebody to set up and stock their motor cars in these parts, and they think I'm the man for the job."

"Well, if that don't beat all," Gavin said quietly.

"They call it a dealership," Dylan said, his voice almost bursting with excitement and pride. "This time next year, I'm going to be the proud owner of the first Ford dealership in Nash County."

"I think that's wonderful," Jodie breathed, and saw in his excitement and dreams a reflection of her own hunger for new things. "Just wonderful."

Dylan turned toward her, and for a moment became almost solemn. "Why, thank you," he said, speaking more quietly than he had all evening. Jodie read the message in his eyes and it made her tremble, for it clearly indicated that her understanding and sharing of his excitement meant more to him than he could say—at least for the moment.

Jodie held his gaze for what seemed the longest while, then when he turned back to answer another question from his father, she noticed that Bethan was watching her. And Moira. Both wore a strange expression, one mirrored almost exactly between mother and daughter. Jodie dropped her gaze, disconcerted by the watchfulness she found there. And the concern.

CHAPTER ELEVEN

ALL THAT WINTER Bethan watched the growing romance between Jodie and Dylan. Watched and held her breath and prayed. She loved Jodie as deeply as a sister, and she positively adored her only brother. But the prospect of what she feared made her heart tremble so, she found it impossible to think on such concerns for more than an instant. So it was not until her mother pointed them out that Bethan was forced to recognize what she had prayed would not happen.

Moira had taken to spending time in bed almost every afternoon, a strange practice for such an active woman. But her joints had begun to bother her. Nowadays Bethan had the habit of tasting the air as soon as she returned from school. The house had a different quality when her mother was having one of her spells. Bethan took to preparing the evening meal, but only after she had gone in and sat on the edge of the bed and let Moira feel in charge by telling her just exactly what to serve and exactly how to prepare it. Often Jodie was there working alongside Bethan, waiting for Dylan to finish work, laughing and filling the big kitchen with her sparkle. If it were not for her mother's ill health, that and the worrisome things she tried hard not to see, Bethan would have called those winter afternoons as close to perfect as she had ever come.

One afternoon in late February, Bethan returned to find the house in the grip of that uncomfortable void. She sighed and pushed the door shut, unwrapped the scarf from about her head, hung up her coat, and climbed the stairs. Outside her mother's room she paused long enough to collect herself and to put on a smile.

She opened the door and said brightly, "It's a perfect day to stay in bed, Momma. I've never known it to stay so cold for so long. And that wind!"

"No day is a good day for bed," her mother sighed, not turning her face from the window. "Especially when it's become a prison."

"Don't you worry," Bethan said, refusing to let her mother's dark mood pull her down. She walked over and settled on the side of her bed. "Soon as it starts warming up, you'll be back to your old self again, just you wait and see."

Moira turned to her then, and even that small motion sent grimaces of pain over her face. She reached over and took Bethan's hand. "Oh, daughter, daughter, what on earth would I do without you to brighten up my days and chase away the shadows?"

Bethan saw the circles under her mother's eyes and knew it had been a bad day. "Should I get your medicine?"

"No, it only leaves my head feeling so foggy I can't find a thought to save my life." Moira inspected her daughter's face. "I do believe old Doc Franklin has it right for once. Your eye has definitely corrected itself."

Bethan's next smile was not forced. "No more eye-patch, then. Not ever."

"Let's hope not." Moira's face settled into graver lines. She said quietly, "I've been thinking about Dylan."

The cold Bethan had left outside somehow crept in then, stealing into her heart and seizing it with icy fingers. Bethan nodded. She had too.

"Have you noticed that he doesn't go to church anymore except when Jodie's there?"

Bethan sighed, and with the sound there came a rushing in of all the worries and concerns she had tried so hard to keep at bay. "And she only goes when her father's there."

Moira gave the tiniest of nods. "I tried to talk with him the other night," she said. "For the third time. Or maybe the fourth. He's a charmer, that one. Soon as I brought it up, he laughed and hugged me and changed the subject."

Bethan did not know what to say.

"I'm worried about this," Moira said. "But I can't tell how much of it is real and how much is my illness. Pain has a way of twisting vision, that I know for certain. So I've decided to say nothing further." Moira looked steadily at her daughter. "She's your friend. Has her heart softened to faith?"

Bethan wanted so to nod her head, to offer the assurance she herself so desperately sought. Surely Dylan would know that it would be wrong for him to make a commitment to one who did not share his belief in God. Even so, the easiest thing in the world for Bethan would be to remain blind to what she feared, and pretend that her hopes and yearnings were simple truth. But she could not. She opened her mouth, tried to avoid the question, but no sound came.

"Is it right that the two of them . . ." Moira's face twisted with a sudden lance of pain. Another tiny shake of her head, then, "No, no, this is not the time, nor am I right to search out what I can't see. I'm just going to have to trust your judgment, daughter. I have no choice in the matter."

Bethan released her mother's hand and rose to her feet. Again she opened her mouth to speak, but the words were just not there. She turned and walked from the room, shut the door behind her, then stood in the hall as though lost in a stranger's house. Finally she drew the world into focus enough to walk to her own room, her feet scarcely able to carry her.

Once her door was shut behind her, the force of the decision she faced sent her to her knees.

All she had to do was to do nothing. Just let this fledgling romance take its course, and Jodie would stay in Harmony. Her best friend would never leave. Bethan's most fervent unspoken prayer would be answered. There was no question in Bethan's mind of how it would turn out, none at all. She had been seeing the looks exchanged by Dylan and Jodie.

No matter how far afield Dylan's questing spirit might take him, he would always return home. Bethan was certain. Dylan's roots ran as deep as her own. Anyplace else he would fade away, just whither and die. And the love she could see growing in Jodie's eyes was so strong, so potent, that it was quenching even her endless desire to flee, to fly. Given the opportunity to go off adventuring with her newfound love from time to time, Jodie would return to roost here in Harmony. Bethan was certain of that also.

Yes, she could keep them—both. Physically. But spiritually? What would they do to each other? Would Dylan influence Jodie toward God? Or would she draw him further away from faith? Could Bethan just stand by and let whatever happened happen? The words *unequally yoked* resounded through her mind and heart, refusing to let her leave it be.

She clasped her hands to her chest, squeezing hard, pressing with all the force she could muster to keep her heart from bursting. Because there was more. To say anything at all was to risk making Dylan terribly angry, as well as severing the threads of friendship with Jodie forever.

Bethan knew that ultimately Dylan must answer to his God, that how he lived his life was his own responsibility. But wasn't it her responsibility to share with him what was clear from Scripture and what she knew of Jodie's view of God?

Bethan remained on her knees for over an hour, her body bent over with anguish, her eyes flooded with falling tears, her soul torn between what she felt she should do and what she would rather do.

Finally she rose, her motions as unsteady and slow as an old woman's. She had to do it, and it had to be done now, before her resolve wavered. Before it was too late.

She had to find Dylan. She had to tell him what was in her heart—all of it.

Bethan reached Dylan's new dealership and let herself in through the back entrance. She found him seated in his small office, gathering up papers from the day's transactions and entering them in the daily journal. His head lifted at the sound of her approaching footsteps. A smile flashed, then was replaced by alarm.

"Momma's not worse, is she?" His eyes seemed to

be trying to read her expression.

Bethan gave her head a tiny shiver of a shake. She swallowed and took the chair placed across the small wooden desk from her brother. She dreaded what was to come, wished it could be done by anyone else but her, and prayed fervently for guidance.

Dylan stilled in mounting apprehension. "What's the matter?"

"Momma's just the same," she said slowly. Her gaze lowered. She could not bear to look into those intense gray eyes. "She's concerned," Bethan started, then had to halt. This is all wrong, she chided herself. She could not put this at her mother's door.

"*I* am concerned," Bethan said and glanced up. Dylan had not moved. The entire room seemed to be holding its breath. "You know I love Jodie like a sister. There is no one I would rather see you spending time with than her. But Jodie goes to church when her father goes, and that is all. Attending church every now and then doesn't make for a life of faith."

She had to stop. It felt as though she had just run an impossible race. Her lungs sought frantically for air. Bethan chanced another look at her brother and saw a man caught in a stillness so complete he appeared to have stopped breathing. Only his eyes reflected life, a tragic light of recognition. As though his gaze cast back the thoughts she struggled to share.

"She shuts her eyes and her heart to everything that goes on in church. She's told me that herself." Bethan had to keep staring at her brother. It was only seeing the depth of his gaze, the level of his concentration, that granted her the strength to continue. "I can see it, Dylan. I watch it happen every time I try to talk with her about faith—about God. I have hoped and prayed that being with you would bring her back, open her up again. But it doesn't seem to be happening."

"No," he murmured, so soft she was unsure whether he was protesting what she had said or agreeing with what she had witnessed.

But she knew if she stopped now she would never finish. The band of emotions about her heart was so tight each word was a painful effort. "It *isn't* happening. You're staying away with her. She's leading you—leading you away from God. But you know in your heart that your faith is too important to let this happen. You *know* this, Dylan. You've known it most of your life. You can't let *anything* take faith away from you. It wouldn't be right—not for you, not for Jodie, not for Momma either."

Then she stopped. It was done. Not well, but it was all she could manage. There was nothing more inside her now but the hollow ache of facing the truth of what she had said and forcing it out.

Dylan stirred slowly, like an old man awaking from a long and troubling sleep. He ran one hand through his thick hair and gave a sigh that went on forever. "You think I haven't been seeing this?"

It broke her heart to see him in such anguish of spirit. She reached out a hand, let it rest gently on his sleeve. But she did not speak. There was nothing else she could say.

"I know you're right," he admitted, his voice so hoarse it sounded like another speaking. "I can't go on like this. I never expected it. I mean, I had no idea how bitter Jodie had become about church and faith. I've wanted to fight what I see in her, deny it. But . . ."

Bethan nodded. She understood. It was so hard to say.

"You're right, you're right," he said, the words almost a moan. "All this time I've just been getting in deeper and deeper." He turned gray eyes fully upon her. "I love her, Bethan."

Bethan could not stop the tears. They spilled upon her flushed cheeks. "I'm so very, very sorry," she managed.

He reached his other hand across to hers, gripped it with a frantic strength. "What on earth am I going to do?"

Bethan shook her head. Her heart cried a litany, *if only, if only*, and it seemed as though the very air held still, filled with the moment's grief. "Pray," she whispered. "Pray for God to show you. I don't know of anything else we can do."

CHAPTER TWELVE

BETHAN FUMBLED WITH the lock, spurred by an urgent rapping on the heavy kitchen door. But her hands were trembling so hard they had trouble working the bolt. The rapping grew louder still, and Bethan became fearful that the noise would awaken her mother. When finally she managed to draw back the lock, the door shuddered open as though it shared the dread she felt herself.

Jodie stood there, a light shawl thrown carelessly over her shoulders. The fringed edge whipped in the brisk winter wind that also tore at her disheveled hair. She was beyond distraught. Her eyes were red from weeping, her tear-stained cheeks glistening in the pale glow of the back porch light.

Bethan caught her breath at the sight of her friend, fear a lance in her heart. "Jodie," she said, the word a gasp, and drew her into the kitchen's warmth.

"Is he here?" Jodie's voice shook so hard the words tumbled upon one another.

"Dylan? No." He had come in late, spent the night tossing and turning, and left before dawn. Bethan knew this for certain, as she had lain awake and listened to it all.

Jodie's response was to throw herself into Bethan's arms. Bethan could only hold her and pat the shaking shoulder with a still-trembling hand. She swallowed and managed, "Tell me."

"Dylan," Jodie said, then stopped. She pushed herself back and fought for control. She was stifling sobs as she fumbled in her pocket for a hankie. Bethan handed her a clean simple linen from her own pocket. Jodie blew and dabbed at the tears on her cheeks. She looked at her friend and said, "I don't want him to know I came."

Bethan nodded agreement. That was a sentiment she perfectly understood.

"I was afraid he'd already be back. Maybe I hoped . . . I don't know." She struggled to draw a steady breath and almost succeeded. "No. If that's the way he wants it, then good riddance."

"Oh, Jodie," Bethan whispered.

"He said that he wouldn't be calling on me. Not ever again." Her chin trembled, and one tear escaped to roll down her cheek. But she dragged in another breath and managed to hold to her control. "He said we have to stop seeing each other. That it's all over between us."

"I'm so sorry," Bethan murmured.

Jodie stopped to take a long look at her friend's face. "You don't sound surprised. Don't tell me he told you about it first."

"I'm truly sorry," Bethan repeated. "I prayed and prayed it wouldn't come to this. But . . . but it really . . ."

Surprise managed to clear Jodie's eyes. "What are you talking about?"

"Come and sit down," Bethan hurried on. "I'll fix some tea and we can talk—"

But Jodie pushed the hand off her arm. Her eyes were

beginning to gleam with an emotion other than distress. "Bethan Keane, did you know about this?"

"Well, I . . ."

"Did you?"

Bethan was unable to look into those dark eyes and face the anger they held. She swallowed and licked at dry lips. She said slowly, "He had no choice."

"He talked to you?"

For a moment Bethan hesitated. But she had to be truthful. "We . . . talked," she admitted, swallowing hard again.

"You *knew*." The words were clipped.

Bethan found tears now forming in her own eyes.

"And you . . ." The blaze of anger in Jodie's face nearly choked off the words. "You think that he's *right*." It was not a question. It was a condemnation.

"He can't . . . he can't marry outside the faith." Bethan slowly raised her gaze, pleading with her eyes and her voice. "Jodie, you've changed. You don't go to church, you don't pray, you've pushed God—"

"And I thought you were my friend," Jodie said between clenched teeth and took a step away.

"I am," Bethan cried, and felt as though all the pain and hurt Jodie had arrived with had been stabbed into her own heart. "I pray for you every night. I—"

"Don't bother," Jodie hissed. "I don't need your prayers. I don't want your prayers. I don't—"

"Jodie, please."

"I suppose *you* told him that he had to be rid of me," she said in icy tones, belying the fire in her eyes.

Bethan stood mute. There was no point in arguing about how or what she actually had said. But she couldn't admit to it either—hearing it from Jodie's mouth made it sound so wrong.

"I thought we were friends," Jodie said again, biting off the words.

"Jodie, believe me, this has nothing to do—" Bethan suddenly was weeping so hard she could hardly continue. "I love you like a sister—more."

The contempt in Jodie's face was worse than the anger. Bethan took a step toward her, but she spun on her heel and headed for the door.

"Jodie, please. Don't leave like this. Please."

Jodie whipped open the door, then wheeled about. "I thought you were the *one* person I could count on. And that perhaps Dylan would love me enough . . ." She shook her head violently, casting off bitter tears. "I see I was wrong. All wrong. There is no real love in this whole sad, sick world. And don't try to tell me about your loving God. He has never loved me. Never. He took my mother. He took Dylan. And now . . ."

She did not say the word "you." But Bethan knew. The unsaid word hung in the air between them.

"Jodie, please."

"It was *your* choice." Jodie's voice was as cold as the wind blasting in through the open door. "Your choice to end our friendship. Something tells me that wasn't all, though. You had to do the choosing for Dylan as well." She stepped into the darkness, stopped once more, and said, "I never want to see you again as long as I live. Never."

CHAPTER THIRTEEN

THERE WAS VERY LITTLE of spring's gentle transition. The cold continued through the third week in March, and then was followed by some of the hottest early weather anyone could remember. Jodie walked the lane back toward school beneath trees which appeared to have exploded into bloom. Every street, every garden in Harmony was a riot of color. She scarcely noticed it at all.

The school was strangely silent as she let herself in and walked to the principal's office, where she had been told to make an appearance. She knocked on the closed door, and at the sound of the muffled voice, she swallowed nervously and let herself in. "Hello, is this, I mean, are you—"

"Yes, yes, come in and shut the door." The woman wore a brown dress of heavy weave; it looked uncomfortable and scratchy in this sudden hot weather. Jodie watched as the woman shifted with the impatience of someone who was both overtired and overhot. She also refused to meet Jodie's eye—a bad sign. The woman sighed noisily as she opened the file in her lap, read a moment, and only then raised her head to look—not at Jodie, but at the chair in front of her. "Sit down, please."

Jodie did as she was told, struggling to keep her sink-ing feeling at bay. She licked dry lips with a tongue that felt like sandpaper.

"My name is Mrs. Roland. I am Assistant to the State College Admissions Director, which means I am respon-sible for interviewing candidates." The words were spo-ken in a distant monotone. She shifted again and said with genuine irritation, "I have been traveling now for four solid weeks, and did not bring a *thing* suitable for this hot weather. I had expected to be home long before now." She sighed, clearly displeased with this disruption of her schedule. "But after the Chancellor received your letter, he contacted me himself and told me to come by."

Jodie's throat was too parched to reply. She gripped her hands together in her lap to keep the trembling from showing and gave a single nod. Which was lost on the woman, as she still had not looked directly at Jodie.

"Your records are very good, Miss . . ." She had to stop and search the top of the page before she could add, "Harland. But I must tell you, the application request has reached us quite late. Not to mention the fact that you are interested in scholarship assistance."

"Something . . . something came up that I thought might change my plans," Jodie said miserably, her voice barely audible. She did not wish to even refer to the dreams, the plans, much less explain the situation.

"Very good indeed," the woman continued, ignoring her. "And the written reports from your teachers are equally impressive. Especially the one from, ah, yes, here it is. Miss Amanda Charles." One long strand of dark brown hair escaped from beneath her flat bonnet and plastered itself to her cheek. Impatiently the woman turned over the letter from Miss Charles, read a moment longer, then sniffed and spoke to herself, "I do so wish these village teachers could learn to write without hyperbole. They do absolutely nothing for their students' chances by such blatantly exaggerated praise."

Jodie felt a sudden flush rise of irritation. She kept from snapping out a retort only by biting down hard on the inside of her cheek. Miss Charles was the most honest person Jodie had ever met.

The woman sighed her way back to the front of the folder and read over Jodie's application once more. "Chemistry. How odd. Not to mention requesting the Lerner scholarship. You realize, of course, that the Lerner is given only to two students each year."

This time Jodie did not even bother to nod. The woman's tone said it all. Jodie should not be even wanting to study chemistry, much less applying for the scholarship. The sinking dejection solidified into a leaden ball in her stomach.

The woman plucked a lace handkerchief from her long brown sleeve and glanced out the room's single window as she wiped the perspiration from her face. "I do so wish it would go ahead and storm. Every single afternoon this week, it has seemed as though I'm being forced to work in an overheated smokehouse."

Jodie remained absolutely still. She had no desire to trade comments about the weather with this lady. It was hard to maintain her control, but she refused to give the older woman the satisfaction of seeing how upset she was.

The woman stuffed the handkerchief back out of sight and gave Jodie a patently false smile. "Your records would certainly earn you a place in our English program. Or languages. French, perhaps. Or even Greek, if you are so inclined. There are several church organizations which offer partial scholarships for young ladies such as yourself who wish to become teachers."

"No, thank you," Jodie said coolly, taking great satisfaction in the steadiness of her voice.

Mrs. Roland gave her a sharp look. "And why not, might I ask?"

"Because," Jodie replied. "I am going to study biochemistry." Although how she was going to accomplish that now, without a college enrollment, much less the scholarship, she could not afford to think about. Not now. Not until she was out of here and away from this woman.

The woman examined her for a long moment, then returned to the folder. Her chair complained as she shifted position again. "Biochemistry," she said slowly, penciling something in the margin of Jodie's application. "You realize, of course, that you would be the only young lady within our entire chemistry department." When Jodie did not respond, Mrs. Roland raised her head once more. "And just what is it about biochemistry that appeals to you so?"

"It is the best initial degree I can obtain," Jodie answered, "to go into bacteriology."

The woman and her pencil became utterly still. Then she said, "So what can you tell me about bacteriology as a field?"

Jodie wasn't sure if the woman really wanted an answer, but she decided to seize the opportunity before she was brushed aside with another offhand comment. "It began in the middle of the last century," Jodie began slowly, cautiously, watching her listener. "Louis Pasteur demonstrated that fermentation was not an instantaneous process, but rather was a natural result of bacteria multiplying when granted access to air. His research led to the development of a vaccine against rabies, and the treatment of milk to prevent it from carrying disease."

Mrs. Roland leaned forward in her chair. When she did not speak, Jodie continued, "Robert Koch, working in Germany, used Pasteur's methods to study anthrax. He was the first to develop systems for staining, fixing, and culture, which allowed bacteria to be seen and studied. He went on to identify the tuberculosis bacillus. In this country, Howard Taylor Rickets studied typhus."

Jodie was warming to her subject, and her voice grew animated in spite of her tension. "Joseph Lister is using his work and Welch's study of gas gangrene to revolutionize surgery. In Russia, Elie Metchnikoff has successfully shown how white blood cells are the body's defense against infection. That is where my primary interest lies."

There was a moment's silence before Mrs. Roland murmured, "How remarkable."

"Yes." Jodie's enthusiasm carried her on, her voice now impassioned over the enormous advances in her chosen field. "Metchnikoff demonstrated how polymorphonuclear leucocytes can be seen under the microscope to actually ingest bacteria into their cytoplasm. Not only that, but it has now been proven that some bacteria actually produce toxins, to which the body develops natural antitoxins. This means that the body defends itself both in a cellular and humoral—or chemical—fashion. Emil von Behring has taken a child suffering from diphtheria and treated it with the antitoxin from another patient. The child recovered. This is revolutionary. It means that a lot of other diseases might be treatable with natural antitoxins."

Jodie stopped herself then. But her mind had been awakened and leapt off in a dozen different directions. Just as it always did when she started discussing what she had been reading and studying. But if she kept talking, she knew her disappointment at being rejected would only be worse. She would be even more exposed than she already was. Because the next thing would be to talk about how desperately she wanted access to a laboratory. And to other people who shared her interests. She might even reach the brink of confessing just how lonely she was here, how cut off she felt from the world and all that was happening. Especially now—now that she did not have a friend with whom she could share her hopes and dreams and hungers. But Jodie did not want to speak of that. So she clasped her hands together and waited as the woman's pencil scratched across the paper.

Finally the woman looked up once more, and Jodie realized that the hostility was replaced with genuine interest. "The scholarship board is scheduled to meet only once more this spring, Miss Harland, and that shall take place in one week's time. I would strongly urge you to come to Raleigh and allow them to meet with you personally. Can that be arranged?"

"Yes," Jodie said, suddenly having difficulty finding air to draw into her lungs. "Oh yes."

CHAPTER FOURTEEN

BETHAN HESITATED OUTSIDE the apothecary entrance. She always had to stop at this point, catch her breath, and pull herself together. Here it was, already the end of the summer, and still she had not accustomed herself to this rift with Jodie, her absence from Bethan's life.

Some nights she woke up, her pillow wet with tears she had shed while dreaming, and wondered how she would ever manage without her best friend. She had run the scenes with Dylan and Jodie through her mind a thousand times. She never found a satisfactory answer as to how she might have done it differently. Better, yes—no doubt she could have said it better. But would it still have turned out the same? Such nights always ended with the wish that once, just that once, she had been smarter, had possessed some of Jodie's intelligence, and had known how to do things just right.

It had been a difficult summer all around. Dylan had alternated between needing her comfort and support and withdrawing into icy silence. Her father had been caught up in some big statewide project to teach farmers new methods and was gone almost all week long. And her mother's health had not improved; if anything, the heat had seemed to worsen her ailment. Moira's joints had continued to ache, her fingers and elbows and ankles and knees swelling up at times to nearly twice their normal size.

And Jodie . . .

As long as she could remember, Jodie had always been there for her. Whenever there was bad talk or unpleasant news or struggles which threatened to overwhelm her, Jodie had always managed to be the strength Bethan never felt she had enough of, the one to whom she could always turn. And now she was alone. Bethan's body felt wounded by the pain of her heart. It was as though she had lost a limb. And the only solace she knew came during her times of prayer.

Bethan gathered her courage and pushed open the apothecary door. Her nostrils instantly recognized all the smells she associated with Jodie and her questing spirit. She gave as brilliant a smile as her quaking heart would permit and said brightly, "Good afternoon, Mr. Harland. It's me again."

Nowadays Parker Harland wore the same gray sweater summer and winter, as though he had somehow managed to draw away from the seasons as well as most everything else. He peered over the top of his half-moon spectacles and mumbled, "Afternoon, Bethan." His words were not slurred, rather just poorly put together, as though there wasn't enough emotion behind them to give them proper shape. "Your mother doing any better?"

"Afraid not." She doubted that he cared much one way or the other. But the usual exchange helped ease her own nerves. "The only thing that seems to help any these days is when I rub her with that liniment of yours. Can I have another bottle, please?"

He was already reaching behind the counter. He put down the bottle, rolled it up in brown wrapping paper, twisted the top into a tight curl, then said, "That will be seventy-two cents."

"I am much obliged," Bethan said. She peered into the back room, as she had every visit over the past five months. Jodie was not to be seen. Bethan took a steadying breath. This time she would simply have to ask. "Could I have a word with Jodie?"

For an instant the indefinite fog which surrounded Parker Harland disappeared. A sharp gaze reached out from the years before his wife's illness and pierced her. "You mean to tell me that Jodie did not tell you?"

"About what?"

"If I told her once, I told her a thousand times. This silly quarrel has gone on far too long." Parker Harland shook his grizzled head. "That girl thinks I don't notice anything. But I notice plenty. It's just some things don't seem important since . . ." He allowed the sentence to fade away, as though the thought was simply too hard to finish.

Normally Bethan would have tried to say something in consolation. But just then she did not have the strength. Gripping the shelf, she kept her body erect and repeated softly, "Tell me what, Mr. Harland?"

Parker hesitated, then said as gently as his permanent gruffness allowed, "Jodie left this morning for college up Raleigh way."

Bethan managed to stop the gasp in her throat. Jodie was gone. "She did? Of course she did." Bethan kept speaking because it was the only way she could keep from coming to pieces right then and there. "College. In Raleigh. Of course."

She picked up the liniment bottle and began to make

for the door. She was determined to hold on, though the goal seemed at the top of a steep rise. "Well, it's my own fault for leaving it until the last minute. I should have come sooner. I'll not bother you any further, Mr. Harland." Her numb fingers found the door and managed to open it. Sunlight washed over her. "Isn't it just a lovely, lovely . . ."

Bethan let the door close behind her, the little notice-bell sounding shrill and mocking. She forced her legs to carry her down the length of the building to where the dirt alleyway opened up at the corner. Bethan stopped there because she could not go a step farther. She leaned her back against the brick wall and turned her face to the sun. She tried to catch her breath but could not. The air was too full of her sorrow. It was like drawing shards of glass into her lungs, each breath hurt her so.

———— ✿ ————

"What's that you're telling me?" The strange woman named Netty Taskins squinted down from the top stoop in nearsighted hostility. "You're aimin' on doing what?"

"I'm not aiming," Jodie replied, holding on to politeness only because she needed a room. And a bed. The long train ride and the heat and the heavy satchels and the uncertainties were all weighing her down. "I've already been accepted. I am going to study chemistry at the university."

"Well, if that don't beat all, I don't know what does." The woman turned, pulled open the screen door, stepped through, and held it open for Jodie. "A lady chemist. You a suffragette as well?"

"I'm not really much of anything," Jodie replied, following her into the coolness. "Yet."

"My Harry, he didn't hold with women having the vote. Called them suffragettes a bunch of Yankee troublemakers. But he passed on, must be seven years now if it's a day. He probably wouldn't have held with a lady chemist neither, but he's beyond caring now, bless his cranky old soul." The woman had features so pinched they looked pickled. She inspected Jodie with eyes glimmering from within deep folds. "Who's your folks, missie?"

"Parker Harland, up Harmony way. He runs the town apothecary."

"And your momma, what does she think of this chemistry business?"

"Momma passed on when I was fourteen," Jodie replied, fighting off an attack of the old familiar ache. "But I think she'd be pleased. It's Daddy who's the hard one to get around."

"Yeah, them men, they do surely take some convincing." The wrinkles creased into deeper folds as she gave a quick smile. "Reminds me of what my mammy used to say. Best way to convince a stubborn man is to apply a skillet judiciously between his eyes."

Jodie smiled back, liking this curious old woman. "The college said you might have a room for me, Mrs. Taskins."

"Sure do, missie. I surely do." She reached over and took one of the satchels, then stumped toward the stairs. "Always had a wish for education, myself. Nice to see somebody with the gumption to go where I couldn't. Gives me hope for the future. I'm glad the Lord sent you my way."

Jodie had to stop and catch her breath before going into the department store. The doors were steel and glass and taller than any doors in Harmony, even bigger than the church entrance. Inside she could see people moving about, all of them looking so elegant and busy.

"Are you going in?"

Jodie spun about and faced a stern woman leading a child by the hand. Both were dressed in Sunday-go-to-meetin' finery. The woman looked like something out of a magazine, her hair done up perfectly and topped with a snappy little hat with a pair of black feathers. The pearls around her neck looked terribly expensive. Jodie stepped out of the way. "No, ma'am, you go right ahead on in."

"Thank you," she said frostily. She turned to the youngster and held out a hand. "Come along." The door opened and closed, swallowing them up and leaving Jodie alone in the entrance.

She caught a glimpse of her reflection in the shop window. Her floral-pattern dress, so nice in Harmony, looked cheap and tacky here in the big city. Not to mention her pair of hair-combs, or her scuffed high-button shoes. Jodie took a tighter grip on her purse and pushed her way through the big doors.

Once inside, she had to stop and get her bearings. She had never imagined a store so big. Long aisles filled with every imaginable item stretched on and on. People walked around, calmly inspecting the merchandise, looking as though they knew just exactly what they were about. Jodie's feet seemed rooted to the floor.

"Can I help you?"

She swallowed her startled squeak, spun about, and faced a girl about her own age. Only this one was more done up than the lady outside—hair perfect, clothes new and shiny, and lips painted. Jodie noticed the badge on her lapel and couldn't believe her eyes. This was a sales-girl. She *worked* here.

The young lady's eyes swept over Jodie's clothes and her awkward stance, and she assumed an air of vast superiority. "Did you wish to purchase something?"

"Yes, ma'am." Jodie's voice had shrunk to just above a whisper. "I was only looking for pens and papers and such."

"School supplies are up the stairs and to the left," said the clerk tersely, turning away with a barely perceptible sniff.

Jodie was almost ready to retreat empty-handed when a male voice said, "Don't let her snippiness get your dander up."

She turned and looked up into a smiling face. For some reason the friendliness in his eyes only made her feel more out of place. "I . . . I don't belong here."

"Sure you do. The secret is, don't ever let any of these big-city folk spook you, and if they do, don't let it show." He grinned in conspiratorial fashion.

He had the fresh-faced look of someone raised on the farm. His dark red hair was cut in a style she had already seen around the school that morning while registering, slicked down and parted in the middle. The color perfectly matched the freckles peppering his features. Friendliness and intelligence shone from sky blue eyes.

"You should have seen me my first day last year. I came in here for supplies and had some uppity woman give me what-for, and I still don't know what I did wrong. So I sashayed on out of here, didn't show my face back downtown for a month."

"You're over here at State?"

He nodded. "Only thing that'd ever have gotten me

to the big city." He pointed with his chin. "The section you want is right up there."

"I'm going to be studying at State too," Jodie said, still awed by the fact. It wasn't her normal manner to talk with strange young men, but she had never felt so alone and at loose ends in her entire life. "I just arrived this morning."

"Welcome to the big city. I'm Lowell Fulton." He climbed the stairs beside her.

"Nice to meet you, Mr. Fulton. I'm . . ." Jodie reached the top step and stopped cold. "Oh my," she said as she faced another enormous room full of aisles and merchandise.

"Don't let it worry you. Another week and you'll have this whole place down pat. Now, what was it you were after?"

"The usual school supplies." For one moment Jodie hesitated, then plunged on, feeling that this kind young man would be safe to confide in. "And a slide rule."

Lowell gave a quick laugh. "You want what? A slide rule?"

Jodie nodded. Thankfully her father had finally relented and offered to help her with expenses not covered by the scholarship. As soon as she heard the news, she knew what her first purchase would be. She had wanted a slide rule for years.

"I'm going to be studying chemistry, but I want to take some mathematics too. I want to be able to handle statistics, and . . ." She realized the young man beside her had stopped. Jodie looked at him, then asked, "Is something the matter?"

"Chemistry?" he said, his voice as flat as his eyes. Jodie did not understand, even when he continued coolly, "You're that Harland girl, aren't you?"

"Yes. How did—"

But he cut off her question. "Slide rules are down at the end of that aisle," he said, then turned on his heel and retreated quickly down the stairs, not even giving Jodie a backward glance.

Jodie watched him depart, her mouth open in astonishment. Suddenly the fact that Bethan was not there, not near to help her laugh it off and talk about the strangeness of city ways, nearly overwhelmed her. Such thoughts had been hitting her all summer long, striking when she least expected it, leaving her hollow and aching. And now here she was, on the verge of realizing one of her biggest lifelong dreams, but lonelier than she had ever been in her entire life.

She sighed and started down the long aisle. All the sunlight had drained from her day, even when she held the cherished slide rule in her hand.

CHAPTER FIFTEEN

THE NEXT MORNING, up at dawn, she had hardly slept a wink. It wasn't that there was any lack of comfort to her new lodgings. Netty's clapboard house was tidily kept. But the night had been full of strange sounds, and her thoughts had remained awhirl. So much newness. So little that was familiar.

And so very much alone.

She slid from the unfamiliar bed and began dressing. Though scrubbed until it was spotless, the washstand was rickety and scratched. The room's only mirror was so old the silver had flaked away, leaving a scarred and pitted surface. Jodie gave herself a nervous inspection in what was left of its reflection.

Her eyes looked frightened, her face pinched. Her hair was dark and fastened tight against her head, no modern curl to it at all. Her body was tall and lacking curves to soften the angular straightness. Jodie sighed and smoothed out the little lace collar on her blouse. Her first day of college, and she was so scared she doubted she would even be able to remember her own name.

Jodie stopped before the wooden door with its brass number plate. The college building could have swallowed her little school at home with room to spare, and there were a half-dozen more just like it! There were more students, and more noise, than Jodie would have thought possible in one place.

She felt her entire universe focusing on this moment. Before her dawned an entirely new existence. All her hopes and dreams lay waiting for her beyond that door. Still she hesitated, beset by sudden doubts. What if she was not good enough? What if she had only been fooling herself and Miss Charles? How would she ever bear—

"You aim on standing there, Miss Harland, blocking the door all day long?"

Jodie started and turned to face a familiar figure with hostile blue eyes. Lowell Fulton. Strange she would remember his name. "I'm sorry. I was just . . . is this Professor Dunlevy's class?"

"If you don't know, maybe you don't belong. You ever thought of that?" The challenge came from a second young man, as coldly antagonistic as the first.

Lowell remained where he was. "Didn't you tell me you were a first-year student? This here is sophomore Chemistry."

"I, that is . . ." Jodie swallowed to clear the tremor from her voice. "They told me to start with this class."

A flicker of something came and went in those blue eyes, so fast that if Jodie had not been watching carefully she would have missed it entirely.

Another of his companions said, "Well, let's just hope *they* didn't make a mistake."

Jodie took a step back, watched as a cluster of six or seven young men shouldered past and entered the class.

She overheard one of them say to the first, "That ought to set her straight, Lowell."

Jodie stood there a moment longer, shocked by the coldness of their attitudes. Then she sighed her way through the door and into the class, selecting a seat in the very back row. It appeared that hopes and dreams would have to wait.

Professor Dunlevy proved to be everything she had been hoping for, a man who deeply loved his subject, and managed to share his knowledge and his passion with his students. He was just about the least attractive man Jodie had ever seen, with tufts of graying hair springing out from his head as though he had just applied a severe electric shock to himself. His eyes bulged slightly, and he had what appeared to be a week's worth of lab work on the front of his formerly white coat. But once he started his lecture, all that faded into insignificance.

As that first class session dispersed, he called from the front, "Miss, ah, let me see, what did I do with that slip? Yes here it is, Jodie Harland. I'd appreciate it if you could stay behind for a moment, please."

As the other students filed out, one of the young men passed her seat and muttered, "Leaving us so soon?"

Jodie set her face in firm lines and raised her face to meet his eyes. "No," she replied tightly.

He tried to hold her gaze but could not. Looking disconcerted, he passed on. Jodie kept her face upturned, though it cost her. But to her surprise she did not meet the expected hostility from Lowell. Instead, as he walked by he simply studied her. Thoughtful, uncertain, something again flickering deep within his eyes.

When the room had emptied, Jodie walked to the podium. Dr. Dunlevy waved at a nearby chair. "Have a seat there, why don't you? Just wanted to welcome you properly."

"Thank you," Jodie said, so grateful for the genuine warmth in his voice that the words came out a little unsteady.

"I was there when you came before the scholarship board, but I don't suppose you remember seeing my handsome face out front," he joked.

"I was a little nervous," she admitted.

" 'Course you were, 'course you were." He stacked his lecture papers, or tried to, but a few of them managed to escape and flutter to the ground. Jodie helped him gather them up. "Thank you, Miss Harland." He straightened and went on, "I was impressed with what you had to say. Gave me quite a thrill to hear how—well, I suppose *impassioned* is the proper word—you were about what you hoped to accomplish."

"It was genuine," Jodie assured him. "Every bit of it."

"I believe you." He settled himself down in the chair opposite her own. "I understand you're from Harmony. I know it well. My own family is from Greenville, not thirty miles down the road. It was a grand little town as well. Everybody knew everybody. You couldn't get away with anything, and didn't much want to."

Jodie watched him stretch out those long legs of his and wondered what she was supposed to say. Nothing in her past had prepared her for small talk with a professor.

"Tell me, Miss Harland, how has your reception been from our other departmental students?"

When she did not reply, he said, "You can tell me honestly."

"Awful."

"Figured as much. There's bound to be some resistance to our first female chemistry major. Especially one who's both pretty *and* smart." He leaned closer. "But I'll tell you something about that group, long as you promise to keep it between us. Far as most of them are concerned, there's a grand old difference between their expectations and their abilities. And none whatsoever between their retention ratio and their lapse factor."

She had to smile. "You mean they forget as fast as they learn."

Mobile features folded into an enormous frown. "Now what's the purpose of all my work to become a scientist, if I'm still going to talk so everybody can understand me?" He examined her for a moment, then said, "Have you met Lowell Fulton?"

"Unfortunately."

"Pity. I was hoping to get there before him. Lowell's a special case. He's from the western part of the state, out past Asheville. Good lad, intelligent, honest, hardworking. He was one of the scholarship winners from last year. Had a friend of his, best friend, actually. One of the finalists for this year's scholarship."

"Oh my," Jodie said.

Dr. Dunlevy nodded. "Took it right hard, hearing how a late entry, and a lady to boot, kept his friend from joining him. The other boy's gotten himself a job and intends to save enough to come next year, whether or not he gets the scholarship, so I guess he's made of good stuff and doesn't give up easily. Bright lad, but between you and me, he's not in your league. Not by a mile."

Jodie thought about Lowell and recalled their meeting of the day before. "I had wondered why Mr. Fulton suddenly seemed so angry with me."

"He'll get over it. He'd better. This time at college should be spent making friends and allies, not enemies.

I aim on telling him that very same thing. Otherwise that kind of mess tends to have a real long tail. It can whip around and become your noose without you ever knowing."

"You want me to give him another chance," Jodie said, understanding him perfectly.

"There, you see, I knew you were a smart one the second I laid eyes on you."

Jodie shook her head doubtfully. "I don't know that he'll be interested enough to try—"

"Just give him a little time to get over his disappointment. Once he recognizes your real capabilities, he should come around." Dr. Dunlevy rose to his feet. "I'd rather not have my two brightest students spend their years trying to tear pieces out of each other's hides."

She thanked the professor and walked from the class, decidedly lighter in spirit than she had been when she entered. As she searched out her next class, she reflected to herself that perhaps college would not be so bad after all.

The changes, when they came, were so surprising that Bethan might easily have attributed them to Indian summer.

They started with Dylan whistling as he went about his morning chores. That alone was strange enough to draw Bethan from the stove where she was fixing breakfast. Dylan still disliked his chores around the farm, as pigs and cows never interested him as much as machinery. To have him whistle while he worked, especially before his breakfast coffee, left Bethan wondering if perhaps he was running a fever.

Then Moira appeared in the kitchen doorway. "Good morning, daughter," she said as she moved stiffly into the room.

"Mother!" Bethan could scarcely believe her eyes. "What are you doing up?"

"Thought it was time to try and stir these old bones." Moira held on to a chair for support, her other hand holding the quilted robe about her. She had lost so much weight over the summer that the robe hung on her. She kissed her daughter's cheek. "How did you sleep last night?"

"Me? Fine." Bethan rubbed the spot where Moira's lips had been. Such affection had not often been shown by her mother since the onset of her ailment. "How about you?"

"Better than an old grouch like I've been would ever deserve. I feel like I've done nothing but fight for sleep all summer. But the air was cool last night, and I rested well."

"You're not a grouch," Bethan said quietly.

Moira, ignoring the comment, peered through the back window. "I see that my ears have not been deceiving me after all."

"I don't know what's gotten into him," Bethan agreed, watching Dylan break into song as he slopped the hogs.

"I do," Moira said. "Your brother has fallen for Carol Simmons."

Bethan stared in open surprise. "The lovely little blond girl who sings in our choir?"

"She's not so little, and far more woman than girl." The edges of Moira's lips lifted a trifle. "He came in and told me last night after you went to bed. It appears that our dear Dylan is well and truly smitten."

Bethan looked from her mother out to where her brother was dousing himself at the pump, and back again. "I don't know what to say."

"Well, I most certainly do." Moira straightened as much as her joints allowed and turned to face her daughter full on. "I have spent many a night praying about what happened when you spoke with Dylan about your friend Jodie. I will not tell you that I did not have my doubts. But pain has a habit of speaking falsehoods to the mind. And last night as I looked into my son's excited eyes, I heard from the Lord as clearly as if He had come down and spoken in my ear."

Moira's eyes positively glowed as she continued, "You did right, Bethan. Hard as the choice was, and I know for certain it was one that tore at your heart, I am positive that you did what was appropriate and right. And I am very, very proud of you."

"Oh, Momma," Bethan whispered.

"I am still praying for my 'other daughter,'" Moira said meaningfully as she moved closer to give Bethan a quick, fierce hug. "I also know that if you don't tend to the bacon it's going to sizzle up to nothing."

Bethan turned back to the stove just as the back door opened. "Man, oh man, does that ever smell good!" Dylan stamped his boots on the rug and shut the door. He walked over, a grin stretching his lean face, and gave Bethan a one-armed hug. "How's my little sister doing this morning?"

"Fine," she managed and blinked hard to clear her eyes. "Just fine."

CHAPTER SIXTEEN

TWO MONTHS AFTER her arrival in Raleigh, Jodie returned from class to find Netty in the backyard, bent over a metal washboard and flat-bottomed tin tub set up by the pump. A tall pile of wrung-out sheets dripped on a side table. Netty looked up at Jodie's approach but did not stop feeding sheets through the wringer. "What's got your face pulled down at the edges?"

"I don't believe what just happened to me," Jodie announced ruefully.

Netty humphed once, and it took a moment before Jodie realized she had just seen the woman laugh. "Must be for real, then. The realest is always the hardest to believe."

"They're trying to block me out of the labs. Nobody is willing to be my partner."

"I'm hearing," Netty said. "But I sure ain't understanding. Is this bad news?"

Jodie explained what lab work was and how important it was to her. Netty's face remained immobile as she listened, her eyes squinted up against the sun and the starchy steam rising from the sheets. One hand fed a continual stream of sheets through the wringer while the other cranked the handle that turned the pair of rollers. Bluish water splashed onto the ground at her feet. When Jodie was finished, Netty remained silent as she fed through the last sheet, then pressed both hands firmly against her back as she slowly straightened. Bright bird-like eyes squinted at Jodie. "Seems to me you're missing out on the possibilities here."

"I guess it's my turn not to understand," Jodie answered. "Do you want me to help you hang those sheets out?"

"You stay put, missie. Ain't no good in your getting starch all over them pretty school clothes."

"What do you mean, possibilities?"

"Ain't sure exactly. But if nobody's gonna hang around to share in the work, it means they ain't gonna share in the glory neither."

Jodie placed her books on the ground and settled herself down upon them. "I never thought of that."

"Them teachers didn't get where they were by being dumb. If they see you off doing your best and doing it by yourself, why, they're gonna take note."

"I don't know if I can do it all by myself," Jodie confessed.

Netty lined up clothespins between her lips, whipped the top sheet out with a wet pop, and draped it over the line. She pinned it into place, then said to Jodie, "Appears like you've reached another of them places where it's important to ask the good Lord for help."

Jodie looked at the ground by her feet, unable to confess that she and the Lord were not on speaking terms.

"There, see, you've taken the biggest step already," said Netty, misunderstanding the bent head. She popped open another sheet, draped and pinned, then went on, "Bowing a proud head is a hard thing to do. Asking for help is never easy. Neither is receiving it when help is offered."

Jodie pulled up a handful of grass and tossed it into the fitful breeze. With the dawn had come the first winter frost, but now the late afternoon sun felt almost hot. Not comfortable with the conversation, she asked, "How did you come to be here, running a rooming house all by yourself?"

A pair of sheets were hung on the line before Netty spoke again. "I was the runt of the litter, seventh in line and never much to look at. My daddy married me off to a widow-feller when I wasn't but fifteen years old. Didn't hardly know the man before I was walking down the aisle."

"That's awful," Jodie said quietly.

The wizened face appeared from between the rapidly growing line of sheets. "Not really. That's the way it was done back then. Country folks like us didn't have no hope in quarreling about a decision. When Daddy said we had to do something, well, that was all there was to it."

"Did you love him at all? Your husband, I mean."

"In a way, I suppose—mostly. The Lord tells us to love all our fellow men." Bright eyes glittered at her. " 'Course, the hardest folks to love are the ones always under foot." She popped open another sheet. When the pins were out of her mouth, Netty went on, "We moved up here to the city on account of his business. He was in the lumber trade. Soon after that, he up and died on me. Left me with a heap of bills, a business that he'd barely gotten started, and this big old pile of a house. I was scared, and I was lonely, but I can't say I was all that sorry. I was free for the first time in my life. Got rid of the business soon as I could. That eased the debt burden some. Decided me and the Lord was gonna either make a go of a life on my own, or go down kicking."

Jodie turned at the sound of laughter from the parlor's open window. There were a half-dozen women student boarders at Netty's. All save Jodie were studying to be teachers, but they appeared to be more interested in finding husbands than finishing their schooling. They treated Jodie with the distant courtesy a well-bred lady would show someone from another country. They simply could not understand what Jodie was after, studying chemistry for one thing, and studying as hard as she did for another.

Netty uncurled the last sheet. "You made yourself some friends over there yet?" she wanted to know.

"Not really." Again there was the lancing pain at the word friend. Bethan's absence, and even more the rift between them, remained a wound that twisted Jodie's insides at the most unexpected moments. She said, "Dr. Dunlevy, I suppose, if you can count a professor as a friend. I like him a lot." She hesitated a moment, then added for reasons she scarcely understood herself, "And there's this other student; his name is Lowell Fulton. Half the time he seems to hate me, but every once in a while he looks at me or says something—I don't know, like he's trying to make amends for his coldness."

"He an ambitious fellow? Intelligent, maybe?"

"Dr. Dunlevy says Lowell and I are the two best students," Jodie replied, embarrassed and proud at once. "As for ambitious, I can't say. He's certainly a leader among the other students. They all seem to look up to him."

"I know the type. Seen enough of them around my husband's business. You mind what I'm telling you, missie, and stay away from that one." Netty upended the tub and let the soapy water pour onto the ground. "Fellow like him, he's got himself just one ambition. Don't have to see him to know him. All them early risers out there, they're *ambitious*. But that fellow, now, he's only got himself *one* ambition. He is dead set and determined to rule the roost. He knows you're competition, too. Makes him nervous."

"Maybe you're right." Jodie rose to her feet, brushed off her skirt, and said quietly, "I am grateful, Netty. For everything."

Netty bobbed her head in her quick, birdlike motion. She looked long and hard at Jodie. "Never had me a youngster of my own," she said slowly and Jodie thought that she saw a shadow in the narrowed eyes. "But I'll say this—if ever I'd been graced with a daughter, I'd have thanked the good Lord if she'd been like you."

In her lovely mint green gown that set off her hair and delicate coloring, Bethan stepped into the church. She paused to inhale the fragrance of all the flowers and wondered how on earth they had managed to gather so many lilies in January.

It was so sweet of Carol to ask her to be a bridesmaid. They were not really close even though they did have warm respect for each other, but Carol had the rare ability to understand instinctively what her man wanted. Dylan had reacted with astonished joy to the news that Bethan was to be bridesmaid, all the thanks Carol ever could have asked for. Bethan's own gratitude was another tie in the new family bonds that were being forged by this wedding.

The church was full. Every face turned and smiled as

Bethan preceded the bride down the aisle. It seemed as though Carol's ethereal beauty had rubbed off on all of them today, and even roughhewn country people had a winsomeness they rarely exhibited on their own. Even Moira, not fully recovered from her ailment, looked positively glowing.

Bethan accepted the bride's flowers, stepped back a pace, and carefully dabbed at the tear in the corner of her eye. Though she had come to love Carol dearly, the wedding meant an end to the hope she had held that Jodie would somehow return to faith and that she and Dylan would resume their courtship. Bethan had longed for Jodie to return to Harmony—to become a part of her family. Now this was not to be. "But, Lord," Bethan prayed fervently again, "please bring Jodie back to you, back to her faith, even if she doesn't come back home—"

Bethan's attention suddenly was caught by the new assistant pastor. Had he smiled? At her? In the three months since Connor Mills had arrived, the whole town had been talking about him. How his fiancee had died not six weeks before their wedding day, just over a year ago. How his heart was firmly given to the Lord. How the children of the church seemed drawn to him like a magnet, and how he had the nicest smile anybody could recollect ever seeing.

Connor stood to one side of the wedding party, the black pastoral robes making his hair look even more blond. Their eyes met, and Bethan sensed as much as saw the sorrow he carried. The shared burden touched her heart, making her eyes well up again. She wiped her eyes once more, glad for the acceptance of tears at wedding ceremonies. No one there would ever guess just why she wept.

She turned her attention to the service.

"Do you, Carol Simmons, take this man to be your lawfully wedded husband, to have and to hold, for better or worse, richer or poorer, in sickness and in health, until death do you part?"

"I do," came Carol's reply, her voice bell-like and as radiant as her face.

Bethan was so happy—for Dylan, for Carol, yes, and even for herself. It felt so good to have a reason to smile.

But even that thought drew her back once again to Jodie. If only Jodie were here to share in the moment, it truly would be a perfect day.

CHAPTER SEVENTEEN

JODIE RETURNED TO COLLEGE the week before the fall term was scheduled to begin. There was little to keep her in Harmony. Her father really didn't need her help in the store, and he moved silently about the house, occupied with a world only he could see. He seemed somehow disconcerted by her presence, as though he had become accustomed to his solitude. Which made the summer months difficult, because she wanted to stay at home, out of sight. Any excursion through the town meant she ran the risk of seeing Bethan—or, worse, Dylan and his new wife. She did not know how she would ever manage such a contact. The few times she had gone out had been to see Amanda Charles, who was leaving to take up a position in Winston-Salem, where her fiance had a new job. With Amanda gone, there would be one less thread tying her to Harmony, one less reason to come home. So it was with a sigh of relief that she returned to Raleigh after the summer holidays, to the quiet college halls and her beloved research.

Jodie had spent her entire summer reading of other scientists' findings, delving through the reports of scientific journals. The first day her father had come across her perusing a journal article on immunology, he had glanced at it over her shoulder, then stopped and squinted at the page before looking at her askance. She was growing into someone he neither knew nor understood.

She would have liked to tell him how important she felt this research might someday become. How it had even begun to fill the hollow points of her life, the ones caused by her loneliness and the loss of her mother and the loss of Bethan's friendship. Maybe the loss of Dylan, too. Though time and distance had made her wonder if that could ever have worked. Particularly now when she realized how exciting and fulfilling her studies and research had become. Some days, when she was able to unravel a particularly knotty problem, she even felt if perhaps she had been able to begin work earlier, she just might have saved her mother's life. If not, then perhaps someday she could help to save another young girl from having to face the distress she herself had endured.

"Well, would you look at what we have here."

Jodie almost jumped from the lab stool. She saved her microscope from toppling over with one hand, then snapped, "What do you mean, sneaking up on somebody like that?"

Lowell Fulton approached her lab station, hands open and outstretched toward her. "I'm sorry. I just didn't realize anybody else was here, is all."

"Well, I am." The sharp edge to her voice had been honed now by a full year of isolation. She swept back her hair and again bent over the microscope. "Now if you'll excuse me, I'm busy."

But Lowell didn't respond to her dismissal. "Yeah, so am I. Guess we had the same idea, trying to get an early start on the year's work."

Jodie made a noncommittal noise, wondering what it would take to make him leave her alone. The first day back, and already the unpleasantness was resuming.

But he didn't turn away, just stood watching her for a moment, making her hands unsure of themselves in spite of her resolve to not let his presence affect her.

"I've done a lot of thinking over the summer," he said casually.

"That must have been a novel experience," Jodie muttered.

Lowell acted as though he had not heard. "I was wondering if maybe you'd like to be my lab partner this year."

The surprise was enough to bring her head upright in an instant. "What?"

"Just a thought." His tone was easy, his face clear. "I watched the way you handled your work last year. You came up with some great results. Even old Dunlevy said so."

"And so you thought you could hitch your wagon to mine, is that it?"

A cloud passed over his features, but Lowell shrugged and said, "That's not it at all. I just thought you might be able to use my help."

"*Your* help?" As though his work was better than hers? She could scarcely believe her ears. "Thanks, but no thanks. Now if you'll excuse me, as I've already said, I'm busy."

Jodie turned back to her microscope. Lowell hesitated, started to say something, then turned and walked away. But she could not concentrate on the task at hand. Imagine the nerve, she thought, her chest tight with anger. All last year she had fought against his cold shoulder and the snide comments of the other fellows, and suddenly he thought he could just waltz over and pretend everything was fine. Jodie struggled to push the incident away. But her thoughts did not easily let go. Her memory seemed etched with the look on Lowell's face when she had brushed aside his offer. He deserved nothing better, said one part of her mind. Was he really declaring a truce? another part asked. Why? Was it truly just for his own gain? She did not know him well, had no reason to try, nor any reason to make an attempt. Yet there was something about the whole exchange that did not sit well. Again she fought to concentrate on her lab work. But there remained the unsettling feeling that she had just made her first big mistake of the school year.

Another year had passed with a speed Bethan would not have believed possible. Twenty months after her brother's wedding, another autumn arrived, and the countryside overflowed with sounds. They filled Bethan's world and her heart to bursting. She had always remembered seasons and events first by sound, second by smell, and only third by sight. It was a fact she never talked about with anyone, for fear of ridicule. A summer night was an orchestra of wind and whispering pine and tinkling chimes and crickets. Conversations escaped through open windows, giving porch-sitters reassuring company. Dogs shouted excitedly in the hot distance. Summer was a crowded time for sounds. Winter, on the other hand, was the season of silence and muted tones—softness blanketed by snow, dripping icicles on frosted eaves, gentle tinkling of silvery wagon bells. Each season had its own sounds, its own smells. Together they blended to fill Bethan's senses with Harmony and home. For this reason more than any other, Bethan could never think of living in a city. She would lose too much of her secure circle of sounds.

As always, thoughts of the world beyond Harmony brought Jodie to mind. But Bethan was becoming accustomed to dealing with them, learning how to push them aside before they worked their way inward to where they could cause her real pain. She skipped up to Dylan and Carol's front door, pushed it open, and called inside, "Anybody home?"

"Upstairs," she heard Carol respond.

Bethan climbed the stairs and found Carol changing the baby. She made a picture of happy motherhood as she bent over her little one, eyes so full of love and laughter that they sparkled with intensity. "Can you come hold little Dylan for me?" she asked, half turning to greet Bethan with another smile.

"Gladly." Bethan's heart reached out with her arms as she took the squirming little bundle and nestled him close, filling her senses with his freshness and clean milky scent. As always, looking at that little face for the first time each day was like seeing it anew. "What a wonderful little boy you are," she murmured, snuggling her face into the soft neck.

Carol washed her hands in the basin, smiling at Bethan in the mirror. "I suppose eight months old is really too young, but I do feel as though he can understand you," she said with motherly pride.

"Of course he can," Bethan assured the smiling little child. "He's a special little boy, aren't you? Yes, you are."

Carol walked over, wiping her hands on her apron,

and looked at the two of them. Her eyes smiled, then darkened with seriousness.

"You know," she ventured softly, her tone full of love and concern, "you should be getting out more. You look pale."

Bethan kept her face turned toward the baby, not wanting to reveal how the words wounded. She knew the truth. She did not look pale. She looked awful. She was up all hours, helping her father take care of her mother. Her father still had a job that he did not dare give up, and her mother needed help almost constantly. It was getting to be too much, but there was nothing she could do about it.

She tickled little Dylan under the chin and responded as casually as she could manage. "Momma's had some bad days."

"But you just can't keep going day and night, Bethan. Nobody can."

"Let me get Momma back on her feet," Bethan said with forced gaiety. "Then you just watch how I start stepping out."

When Carol did not answer, Bethan turned and was met by a very concerned gaze. "You're a wonderful daughter and a blessing to the family," Carol said. "All the same, you're about to worry Dylan and me something serious. We fear you're going to work yourself ill. When I come over with baby Dylan to give you an occasional bit of time off, you go grocery shopping or something equally boring." She hesitated, then added, "You're still young. You should spend more time with people your own age. What about that pastor? Connor Mills is a fine young man, and he's spending far too much time alone. I think—"

"Do you know, I believe this baby needs another change," Bethan said, holding determinedly on to her cheerful tone. She handed the baby over and said, "Don't you worry, sister. I'll be just fine."

CHAPTER EIGHTEEN

THE RUN-UP TO GRADUATION was wonderfully exhilarating, and utterly confusing. Around Easter word leaked out that Jodie Harland was walking away with almost every honor, including class valedictorian.

The result was a gradual transformation of her status among her classmates, and deferential treatment from all but a handful of stalwarts. This minority continued to proclaim loudly and resentfully that a woman had no place studying science. But Jodie was finding it easier to ignore them, especially now that so many others sought out her company. Around campus she was being hailed by total strangers. Young men stopped to smile, say hello, and pass the time of day. Young women seemed to take pride in her brains, as though higher intelligence offered them a reason to excuse her unfeminine ambitions.

But it was difficult for her to come out of her protective shell after so long. Jodie's ability to make friendly small talk had become rusty after the time of isolation. Then a journal article written by Dr. Dunlevy named her and Lowell Fulton among the research staff, and the attention sent her way increased even further.

Her contacts with Harmony had been reduced to the

slenderest of threads. She continued to write her father every week. Because the apothecary had its own phone, she placed a long-distance collect call the first Sunday night of the month. But his responses were brief, mumbled replies or an occasional card filled with a haphazard scrawl which she could scarcely read.

To her utter surprise, the week before Easter Jodie found a letter from Moira Keane waiting for her in her school mailbox after classes. Shocked by the name and return address, she tore the envelope open and scanned swiftly. She saw enough to know that one name sprouted from every paragraph. Bethan. Jodie crumpled the letter, amazed that it could still hurt so much. She stuffed it into her handbag with the determination to drop it in the stove once she was home.

But the shock and the memories it unleashed stayed with her, and she soon gave up on plans to work in the lab that afternoon. She started back toward the boardinghouse.

Her second shock of the day came down Netty's front steps as she turned the corner. She was tremendously unsettled to see Lowell Fulton walk out of her home. The sight of him disturbed her little protected corner of the city, leaving her exposed and vulnerable.

But his own face lit up when his eyes spotted her. "There you are. Been having a nice chat with your landlady," he said as he approached. "Back home we'd say she's the kind who likes to make home folks of just about everybody she meets. About the nicest compliment you could give somebody."

He rattled on in easy conversation, but it made her even more uncomfortable to know he had been talking with Netty. She asked coldly, "What are you doing here, Lowell?"

"I just wanted to have a chat with you, someplace away from school," he said, seemingly not put off by her tone. "You're always so busy around the lab and such, I thought it would be easier to speak my piece out here in the open air."

"Well, you found me. What's on your mind?"

He gestured back toward the porch. "Mind if we go sit down?"

Jodie gave her head a decisive shake. "I don't think so."

He peered down at her. "You sure don't make it easy for a fellow."

For some reason she felt the palms of her hands growing clammy. Lowell recently had been sending more and more undesired attention her way. "I asked you what it was you wanted."

He took a breath, let it out slowly. "I was just wondering what you had planned for next year."

For a moment she held back, not sure if she should answer his question. But he looked open and sincere, and before she knew it she found herself volunteering the truth. "I'm not sure yet. Probably go to work for one of the pharmaceutical companies moving into Raleigh."

He kicked at the sidewalk with the toe of his shoe. "Dunlevy's offered me a chance to stay on and do post-graduate research."

"I know." Professor Dunlevy had told her about it himself, and had made the same offer to her. But Jodie was not sure she could endure more of the school's enclosed, male-dominated atmosphere, despite the attraction of doing independent research. "Congratulations."

"I was wondering . . ." He stopped, studied the sky for a long moment, took a deep breath and said, "I was wondering if you'd stay and work with me."

"Work *with* you?" Now she understood what this was all about. "You mean, work *for* you, isn't that right?"

It was Lowell's turn to stare. "I didn't mean anything of the sort!"

But Jodie had already worked up a full head of steam. "I remember the way you treated me that very first day, Lowell Fulton. And how you looked at me all through that first semester, like you wished you could freeze me solid."

His wide shoulders slumped. "That was an awful, awful mistake."

"It sure was." She looked for another handle to grab on to, something to give her a reason to add more fury, but his tone was so abject that she could only say, "A terrible one."

"I'm really sorry, Jodie. I've been sorry for a long time, and I've tried to say it a couple of times, but you— well, I was a coward. I open my mouth, and you're already turning away. I've wanted to apologize for a long time."

"I can just imagine," she said bitterly. But she was suddenly unsettled by memories of certain moments over the past year when Lowell had approached her, or tried to. She had taken pride in how swiftly she had raised the barriers. Even now she was in no mood to listen. She pushed the thought of a reconciliation away and went on, "You were jealous then, and you're still jealous now."

"I'm not going to let you bait me," he said steadily. "I admit I *was* jealous. That was wrong, and I treated you awfully. I am very sorry for that." He stopped for a moment, then said, "Even when I was acting like a selfish idiot, deep inside I admired you, your courage and your skill. Don't you see—?"

"I see, all right," she interrupted, but it was a struggle to keep her anger intact. Something about his sincerity and calm tone undermined her stubborn resolve. "The same person who treated me like bacteria the first time he laid eyes on me."

He winced at that but kept his tone level, his gaze direct. "You are right. I have no right to ask for your forgiveness, but I'm asking anyway."

A sudden flower of pain bloomed at heart level. "What?"

"Forgiveness," he repeated. "I have asked God's forgiveness. Now I'm asking yours." A touch of humor surfaced. "Our Lord said to forgive seventy times seven. I know I came close—but maybe I haven't exceeded that limit yet."

Jodie only looked down at the toe of her shoe, saying nothing.

He went on in a softer, more pleading voice. "It is almost as hard to ask for as it is to give, but that's what I'm doing. I'm truly sorry I hurt you. And got the rest to follow suit. I was a fool. I'm ashamed of what I've said—and done—but I can't undo it. I can only ask you to forgive me and let me have another chance." Another long pause. "Could you find it in your heart to forgive me? Could we be friends?"

Friends. The word pierced her to the deepest level, and suddenly the letter she carried in her handbag seemed to burn against her side. Jodie started around him, her legs unsteady. "No, I can't . . ."

"Jodie, please—"

"I . . . you . . ." Jodie gave up, turned, waved a vague hand, and walked toward the house. She had no desire to be so deeply hurt again.

"There you are." Netty had her ironing board set up in the front parlor as Jodie walked in the door. "Been somebody here looking for you."

"I know." Jodie sank into the nearest chair. "I just saw him."

"That the fellow you was telling me about, the one studying chemistry with you?"

"Yes."

"I was afraid of that." The irons rested on the top of the room's potbellied stove. Netty picked one up with her heat-blackened hotpad, thumped it down on the ironing board, ran it back and forth, then returned it to the stove with a clang. She hefted the next one, tested it with a licked finger, sprinkled water over the tablecloth, and ironed it smooth. Netty looked up, then said, "I fear I made a terrible mistake."

Jodie stared at her. "What?"

"Part of being human, I suppose, but I hate making errors with other people's lives. Especially yours. But I'm afraid I did." The iron was replaced, the cloth folded and another put in its place, and the ironing continued. "I think maybe I was listening to your feelings more than I should have, though it pains me to say it. And maybe meddling in your affairs when I shouldn't have been, mixing my memories with your truth."

"What are you trying to tell me?"

"That I think your fellow is a fine upstanding young man," Netty replied crisply.

"He's not *my* anything."

"He would be if you let him." The iron came down with an authoritative thunk. "Yessir, a good-hearted man and a Christian to boot."

Jodie stared at the pinched-face old woman and felt the axis of her world shift. Netty's words only served to make her feel even more confused. With a catch in her throat, she spoke quietly. "I don't know what to do."

"You'll discover something soon enough," Netty said firmly. "Of that I have no doubt whatsoever."

Jodie thought of Lowell's last words, then remembered all that had preceded them. "I don't see how," she said with a sigh. "It's already over and done with."

"You can stop that right sharp, missie. That gloomy thinking won't get you nowhere but down."

"But you don't know what he—"

Netty shushed her. "I'll give you a bit of advice it took me years to discover. Don't worry on what's past and can't be changed. When your mind tries to bring it up, turn yourself away, unless of course you're looking for a solution. You can do that, you know, turn away on the inside. It ain't easy, but you can do it. Dwelling on past wrongs does nothing but open old wounds when the Lord is trying to heal them up. What's done is done, you hear what I'm saying?"

Jodie nodded once. She heard.

"Life's full of injustice, specially to anyone blessed by being born a woman. You just have to make up your mind to let go whenever such wrongs are done to you. Just let them go, and look on to tomorrow."

Jodie picked at a loose thread in her hem. "I don't know as I would call being a woman *any* blessing. From where I sit, the injustices are winning out."

"That's your pain talking, not your head." Netty propped two work-worn hands on her hips. "How would you like to go through life without a woman's heart? Miss the joy of a sunrise, or birdsong, or a quiet moment of rest and prayer? You just remember what I'm telling you. A woman pays for her blessings by having a heart that stays wide open to both joy and pain." Her eyes glistened with time-sharpened zest. "And friendship. And even love, though it must sound strange coming from the mouth of an old fogey like me. But it's the truth. If the dear Lord chooses to bless your life with love, then be strong enough and *womanly* enough to open your heart and accept it. Take it in deep. Make it grow. Give it your all, as only a woman knows how to do."

Bethan held on to control only because Dylan Junior and baby Caroline needed her strength. Being needed was exactly what the moment required. Otherwise she would be as broken as the little ones' father.

Her brother Dylan made it to the grave site because his father and one of his best friends half guided, half carried him there from the church. It did not matter to any of them that the flu epidemic was all but over. Carol had caught it while still recuperating from childbirth and was gone before the family hardly realized how ill she had become. Her sudden passing had felled Dylan as squarely as an axe.

And Bethan's mother. Moira was going through another of her bad spells, up much of every night with the pain, needing to have liniment rubbed into her swollen joints, taking pain medicine more and more often. It left her slack-featured and frail, not at all ready to handle a crisis like this.

Bethan walked behind the coffin, the tiny infant Caroline in her arms. Little Dylan kept hold of her skirt with one fist, the other grabbing tightly to one of Moira's swollen fingers. The little boy was whimpering softly, but Bethan was not sure just how much his two-year-old mind truly understood. Still, a glance his father's way was enough to paint fresh tears upon the little fellow's cheeks.

A wave of grief, coupled with the additional burden of even more to care for, nearly overwhelmed Bethan. As they settled into the single line of chairs, she lowered her face to the sleeping baby's cheek. She felt weak with pain and tired from constantly being needed. It wasn't like her to feel sorry for herself. But she truly felt as though she had no life of her own at all. Moira required so much help, not to mention the housework and all the extra chores. And now this.

Bethan stroked the silky dark hairs from the baby's forehead, then reached over and drew little Dylan closer to her side. Those two warm, round little bodies were enough to strengthen her resolve and lift her tired shoulders. She would cope. Though she wasn't sure exactly how, what with only twenty-four hours to the day and just one set of hands. Still, her brother and the children were going to need her too in the coming days.

A tall form passed before her, blocking out the sun. She looked up into the face of the assistant pastor. Connor Mills was not smiling now as he lowered himself on a knee in front of Bethan's chair. He reached forward, placed one strong hand on her arm, and said quietly, "You have my deepest sympathy in this moment of sorrow, Miss Keane."

The genuine care and concern in his voice nearly did her in, and it felt as though the dams inside were about to burst. Bethan had nowhere to hide, not with the baby in her lap and little Dylan clinging to her side. So she blinked back the tears and managed to whisper, "Thank you, Pastor Mills."

His gray-green eyes studied her from beneath the

blond hair, so fine and light it looked almost permanently disheveled. He remained there in front of her, his eyes solemn and intent and asked quietly, "Will you manage?"

"I don't see how," she replied truthfully. "But I will—because I have to."

He nodded, as though expecting nothing less. A moment's hesitation, then more quietly still, "Will you let me help you?"

This time the tears could not be held back. But there was more than sorrow pushing them out. Bethan could not understand all the strange emotions that wanted to tumble forth, one behind the other. She raised the corner of the baby's blanket, wiped her cheeks, and gave a slow nod. Sad as the day was, there was a note of hope to be found in the offer of Connor Mills' strength.

CHAPTER NINETEEN

BY AUGUST, EVERYONE in Harmony was thinking of them as a couple. Connor was hale and hearty, his shock of white-blond hair blowing like straw in the faintest breeze. One hand was continually brushing it from his eyes, usually in the midst of an excited discussion with someone. He did everything with his hands, and everything with enthusiasm. Sometimes, when Connor was telling Bethan about a young person converted to Christ or some new program he was planning for the church, she felt as though she were the only thing holding Connor Mills to earth.

The pair of them made people smile, and she liked that. She was happy that those who liked Connor were genuinely relieved he had found her, someone so stable and calm and dependable. And he did care for her; Bethan did not doubt that for a moment. One look into those gray-green eyes, and she had no question that the church's assistant pastor had fallen head over heels in love. With *her*. Bethan could scarcely believe it was really happening. To someone beautiful and talented and smart, certainly. But not to her. Then a look into his face would confirm in her heart what her mind could not.

The first evening in September found Bethan curled up on the porch swing, surrounded by the night. Indian summer had arrived early. The days generally were clear and only warming around noon, while the nights held a chilly note. She pushed herself back and forth with one toe, her shoulders protected by a fine shawl. The swing's gentle creaks were echoed by crickets in the nearby shrubs.

Bethan breathed in deeply, enjoying the time of blissful relaxation from the cares of the day and the duties of the coming night. For now, blest relief, her mother rested quietly.

The night was awash in silver from a brilliant moon suspended within a heaven-wide swath of stars. A shadow flitted from one dark pine to another, followed by the hooting call of a night owl. Bethan drew the shawl closer about her, content and peaceful.

She had nothing specific she could identify as the reason for feeling as she did. But the mood was too powerful to be denied, too pleasing to be questioned. She sighed and pushed the swing as gently as she could and still be in motion, not wanting anything to disturb the graceful wonder of this night.

Off in the distance a train gave its plaintive call, and it reminded Bethan of Jodie. Yet instead of being filled with the sorrow of her friend's absence, of the terrible rift between them, tonight was somehow different. She had never envied Jodie her hungry heart and questing mind. Her friend was far more intelligent, and would most likely rise much further, and would do important things in the world. But would she ever know the peace of a quiet autumn evening shared with a sleepy country town and her Lord?

Bethan raised her face to the stars, inhaled a fragrance

wafted upon the faintest of breezes, and prayed again for her best friend, for she still thought of her as such. "Lord," she whispered more with her heart than her lips, "please wrap your arms around Jodie. . . ."

"Miss Bethan?"

Bethan stopped her swinging and peered out into the darkness. "Connor? Is that you?"

"Yes, ma'am, it surely is. May I join you, please?"

The thrill at the sound of his voice made every fiber of her being come instantly more alive. "Of course you can." There was not the ending of her peace, but rather a shifting, as though the inner gift were making room for him as she did herself upon the swing. "What has you talking so formal tonight?" she teased lightly. "You'd think we'd never met, instead of sitting in church together just yesterday."

Connor climbed the front stairs, passing into the soft glow of light sifting through the screen door. He wore his best dark suit. His blond hair was carefully brushed. His hands held a hat in front of him and made a continual nervous revolution as he approached.

Bethan inspected the tense features, the overbright eyes, the set to his shoulders, and felt her pulse quicken. She stopped her swinging, settled both feet down together upon the porch, and whispered, "Oh, my."

"Miss Bethan, I'm here to tell you how much I care for you," he said, speaking in an uncharacteristic monotone, as if he had practiced so often the words had been drained of all feeling. Despite the evening's chill, perspiration made his forehead gleam in the soft light. "How much I care for you," he repeated, this time his heart filling each word with emotion. "I am asking you to be my wife, Bethan Keane. Will you marry me?"

"Oh, Connor." Her voice was suddenly as light and

soft as the evening breeze. "Of course I will."

"What?" Connor's own voice had fallen to a level matching her own.

For some reason Bethan could scarcely catch her breath. She whispered, "I said yes, Connor. I would—"

A voice with a faint Welsh accent was heard from the second-floor window. "Speak up, daughter. I can't be hearing what your answer is."

"Momma?" Bethan scrambled to her feet, hurried to the side of the porch and looked up. "What on earth are you doing out of bed?"

"I'm waiting to hear if you've got the good sense to tell that gentleman what he ought to be hearing." Moira pushed up on the window until it surrendered and opened far enough for her to put her head out. "Now answer the good fellow so we can all get our rest."

"I already did, Momma." Bethan laughed and looked back over to a confused-looking Connor. "I told him yes."

"Well, glory be." Moira's head disappeared, and the curtains flicked back into place. "Bid the gentleman a gracious good evening from me as well," she said.

"Yes, Momma. Good night, Momma." Bethan smiled and walked back to where Connor stood stock-still and bewildered. "It's all right. She won't be bothering us any further."

"Maybe . . . maybe I should be leaving," he stammered.

"Nonsense. Come join me on the swing." She graced him with a smile from the heart. "After all, how often does a girl get a proposal from the finest man in town?"

"I'm not that," Connor said, settling down beside her. "But just being with you makes me feel that way."

She took his big hand in both of hers. My husband,

she thought, and felt as though her heart would break free of her ribs. "I think my heart has been waiting for you to come all evening."

"I'll try hard as I know how to make you a good husband."

She looked into the face she had come to love over the months, and she saw that same love mirrored in his eyes. She was amazed at her own calm. All her life she had dreamed of a fine young man telling her those words. Now that it had happened, she felt surrounded by a certainty, a peace, so strong there was scarcely any room for nerves. "I know you will," she assured him. "Your heart is too good to do anything else."

In the faint distance the train whistle echoed yet again, and suddenly the earlier whispers carried by the wind came clear to her mind. Bethan shivered. Perhaps this would be the answer she had prayed over for so very, very long.

"Are you cold, darling?"

Darling. The word was so unexpected that it took a moment before she realized it was meant for her. For *her.* "No, just happy." She leaned her head against his shoulder, felt his strength and his solid presence. Tomorrow she would write the letter, and already she knew just exactly what she was going to say. "So very, very happy."

Jodie had spent the summer suspended between two worlds.

Because of pressure on him to prepare another paper scheduled for presentation at a September conference, Dr. Dunlevy offered her a temporary position as lab technician. She accepted with vast relief. The stipend would grant her enough money to travel back and forth each weekend to Harmony. The job saved her from the need to spend another whole summer hidden away in the too-quiet house, with only her books for company. And the work granted her a chance to see if she wanted to stay at the university and do pure research.

It was easier than she had expected to avoid Lowell. He worked in another lab, and it looked as though he did his best to stay out of her way as well. She tried to convince herself that this was a welcome development but was not very successful. Twice she had thought to start a conversation, only to lose her nerve at the last moment. After that, she simply avoided him and the shadows in his eyes.

Jodie's work with Dr. Dunlevy was beginning to open up possibilities of success and recognition for her. Neither had yet arrived, but both were close enough for her to realize they might soon be a part of her daily life.

Several pharmaceutical companies were moving into the area, setting up labs and factories. She was being courted by three of them. Someone dropped by several times each week, chatting with her, showing they were friendly people to work with, remembering at the last moment that they had thought of something else to offer. The generosity of their proposals were both gratifying and frightening. How should she decide? Dr. Dunlevy wasn't much help. "Go for the biggest money," he joked, when all the while Jodie knew that wasn't high on his priorities.

At the same time, under Dr. Dunlevy's prodding, the college had offered her a part-time research and teaching position, which would give her time to write and present her Ph.D. thesis. The idea of becoming *Doctor* Jodene

Harland appealed more than she liked to admit.

But there were problems as well, questions she would not have dreamed could still be nagging at her. Despite her growing success—more money of her own than she had ever had in her life, stimulating and challenging work under the direction of a man she deeply admired, and the flattering knowledge that major companies in her field were "fighting over her"—Jodie found herself no closer to happiness than she had ever been. Hollow dissatisfaction ate at her, at times stronger than ever before; it seemed as though she felt threatened by success. As though it stripped away a part of her defenses, left her open to a deeper examination of herself than was comfortable.

"Jodie?"

She started from her reverie, turned, and saw Lowell Fulton standing in her open door. "Yes?"

"I didn't mean to frighten you."

"You didn't frighten me," she said flatly, feeling the automatic barriers rise inside her.

" 'Course not," he agreed quickly. He did not seem to be in any hurry, leaning against the doorframe now, glancing around the lab. "How's your work coming along?" he asked.

"Fine," she said, the monosyllable hanging in the air between them. She wondered why she felt so vulnerable whenever he was around. She toyed with the pencil between her fingers and found herself wishing she could let go of the past and accept his offered friendship. She needed him. At least, she corrected herself, she needed *someone.*

But the old resistance to new friendships was not so easy to dismiss. "I thought," she said, the same old coldness in her voice, "that you were working under the same deadline for your results as me?"

"Oh, that tobacco's been barned," he said easily.

"Pardon me?"

"Finished up the project four, five days ago."

Once again, there was the sense of Lowell catching her totally off guard. Jodie looked down at her own results. She had another week's work to complete. At least.

"I was just wondering," Lowell went on, "if you'd decided what you were going to be doing come the end of this month."

"Not yet," Jodie replied.

"You know, those companies have been after me as well," he went on. "Been thinking maybe it'd be good to get my feet wet in the real world, then come back for more schooling. How about it?"

It dawned on Jodie that he knew more about her life than she did about his. "You mean, you still want to work with me? You're suggesting that we team up?"

"Could be," he said, his tone still easy.

Before she could reply, he pointed at her desk. "How do you find anything in that jumble?" The question was asked without rancor, and Jodie decided not to be defensive.

"A messy desk is the sign of a brilliant mind," she replied, but the sharpness was gone from her voice.

"Maybe so," he responded mildly, "but it also makes for questionable lab results. And it slows you down something awful."

While she was still struggling to come up with a response, Lowell walked over and sat down across from her. "I think we should join forces," he told her, his voice quiet yet serious. "I am methodical, you are not. But I lack your vision—and maybe even a little of your insight."

It was quite an admission, without putting himself down. They both knew he had a brilliant mind, so there was no use denying the fact.

Then to Jodie's surprise he looked directly into her eyes and said with quiet honesty, "And I want to share in your glory, plain and simple."

The open guilelessness of his voice disarmed her. "What glory?"

"The glory that is bound to come your way," Lowell answered. "You are too gifted to be held down. Sooner or later you are going to make a discovery that will change the way we live our lives. I can feel that in my bones. But you need me, and if you gave yourself half a chance, I think you'd realize this too. Your lab results— well . . . are sloppy. You are impatient with people who don't catch on as fast as you do. You need me to help deal with the administrators, to talk to the outside world, to write up your results."

He stopped. He must have given the matter a lot of thought. When Jodie did not protest loudly at his words, he leaned across her desk and said with enthusiasm, his eyes sparkling at the very thought, "Jodie Harland, if we were to join forces, there is nothing on earth that could stop us. Nothing."

The moment seemed suspended in time. Jodie had no idea how long she remained there, held by his gaze and the lingering power of his words. Finally she managed, "I'll think about what you've said."

A cloud passed over his face. "Sure you will," he said, his tone now resigned. She knew that was not the answer he had hoped for. He rose to his feet, started to turn away, then remembered. "Oh, I almost forgot. There was a letter in your box. I saw you were busy and brought it over to save you the trip."

"Why, thank . . ." The words faded to nothingness as Jodie saw the name on the envelope's return address.

Bethan.

"What's the matter?" Lowell leaned over the desk, a concerned expression on his strong features. "You look like you've seen a ghost." She still had not taken the letter from him.

"Please don't go," Jodie said through stiff lips. She looked back at the letter, knew she did not have the will to open it, knew she could never throw another one away. The nights after burning Moira's letter had been the worst since her argument with Bethan.

With a trembling hand she pushed the letter away and whispered, "Will . . . will you read it to me?"

Surprise registered on Lowell's face. He sank into the seat opposite her. "Do what?"

Jodie picked up the letter again and extended it across her cluttered desk. "Please."

Slowly he accepted the letter, his eyes fastened on her face. "You've gone all pale. Is it family?"

She shook her head, a quick little tremble.

He glanced down at the letter. "From Harmony. That's your hometown."

Fear left her unable to speak. She had never felt so exposed, so helpless, not in years. For a terrible moment she imagined him tossing the letter back to her, responding with the same coldness she had shown him. And she was just too vulnerable, too shattered to bear it right then. She needed his help. But all Lowell did was glance once more at her face before slitting open the envelope and pulling out the letter. He flattened it on the edge of her desk, cleared his throat, and began to read aloud.

" 'Dearest Jodie. I have the most exciting news, and I simply could not keep it to myself. I am to be married!

Honest. And to the most wonderful man. His name is Connor Mills. I wish I had time to tell you about him. I could write pages and pages about him, but it is late afternoon, and I am already behind in getting the evening meal. Momma has had another bad day.' " Lowell paused and looked up.

Jodie's thoughts whirled within her. The words were in the same simple pattern that Bethan spoke in, and even though they were said by a deep male voice, it still felt as though her friend had entered the lab office and was standing there over her desk. Her *friend*. Thinking of Bethan again opened all the old wounds. And yet there was a difference, a sense of beckoning. Jodie blinked back the tears with difficulty and concentrated on the words as Lowell continued reading.

" '. . . of course I can think of no one but my dearest friend to be my bridesmaid. I would be so honored if you would accept. We have not finalized the date, but we do not wish it to be a long engagement. Is there a time that would work best for you? I will keep you posted. Please, please, if you have a moment, do write and let me know if you could come.'

" 'I must run. Momma is calling.'

" 'With my love, Bethan.' "

In a daze, Jodie watched Lowell fold the letter carefully and look again at her. She found in his cautious gaze the anchor she needed to maintain control. She realized that he had no idea why this letter had affected her so, but seeing the emotions playing across her face no doubt kept him from asking.

She took a careful breath, one which hurt her to draw. Her eyes were ready to spill over at any moment, in spite of her determined effort. She knew she could not speak, not yet, so she made do with a small smile and a nod of thanks.

Lowell took it as a nod of dismissal. He slid the letter back in the envelope, set it on the desk in front of her, and rose to his feet. At the doorway he stopped and turned back. There was a long moment of hesitation before he said quietly, "If you need anything, I'll be down in my office."

She swallowed and tried to form the words *thank you*, but the power of speech had not yet returned. Her eyes drifted down to the letter there before her, and a single hot tear escaped to trickle down her cheek.

Lowell watched her a moment longer and said quietly, "Anything at all." Then he left.

CHAPTER TWENTY

JODIE SAT ON THE SWING beside Bethan, more unsure of what to say or do than she had been in her entire life. Bethan, however, seemed utterly at ease, as if they were girls again making daisy chains. Bethan rocked them back and forth and told in matter-of-fact tones all that had happened in the past few years—Dylan's marriage and the babies, Carol's death, her mother's illness, Connor's arrival, their growing romance and engagement.

Jodie sat and listened, wondering at how calm and contained Bethan sounded. She had been through so much. There was a lot Jodie wanted to tell as well, but not yet. It would be so good to have someone to talk to, someone who would really understand, feel her feelings, take on her struggles, rise up with her joys. Even so, for the moment it was enough to listen and come to terms with this sudden change. One moment, one simple letter, and her entire world was altered.

Finally Bethan stopped, and they spent a long moment rocking in silence, listening to the evening. "It must all sound so . . . so ordinary to you," Bethan said eventually.

That was not what Jodie had been thinking. She realized that Bethan had tasted more of life—the bitter and the sweet—in the intervening years than she could have dreamed of in her protected, isolated corner of academia, all wrapped in self and high ambitions.

"The small-town life of a simple country girl," Bethan finished with a rueful sigh.

"You're not simple," Jodie said quietly, speaking for the first time in a long while. "And you're not a girl. Not anymore."

"No, I suppose not." Bethan continued rocking them steadily. "I guess I've had to grow up. Having Dylan's children need me meant I couldn't hold on to my silliness."

"It sounds like you've really been through the wringer." The image of Netty's wet sheets forced between the rollers, draining, crushing, came to Jodie's mind. Was that what had happened to Bethan? Had all of her little-girl dreams, her childish sweetness, been wrung from her life? Jodie shivered in spite of the warmth of the night.

"I don't mind telling you, Jodie, life has been hard," Bethan agreed quietly. "But I've had the Lord with me through the good times and the bad, and now I have Connor."

Yet there was no sign of crushing, breaking. Bethan spoke with a new sweetness, a new depth in her soul. It was a change brought about by yielding, growing. For one brief moment Jodie, with her aspirations of greatness, almost envied the woman beside her. Would her life have been different if she had handled the pain with less struggle?

Jodie almost missed the swift little glance Bethan gave her under the porch light. "Do you remember Kirsten Sloane?"

"How could I forget." Jodie stirred herself back to the present and gave a short laugh at the memory of punching her into the middle of Harmony's Main Street. "Big girl, not overbright, she used to like bullying you. I always thought she got away with murder because her mother was a teacher."

"Her mother passed on a while back. Kirsten began coming to church soon after. We've started a little Bible study."

Jodie could not help but gape. "You and Kirsten?"

"There are more of us now, usually about a dozen. We meet either here or at Kirsten's every Wednesday. You ought to come."

"Well, if that doesn't beat all." Jodie turned her head back to the night. "Bethan Keane and Kirsten Sloane becoming friends."

"Yes, friends in the Lord," Bethan repeated quietly. "She is a very different person than she used to be—from the inside out. Anyway, she's started coming by and helping me out at Dylan's. The children love her." There was another little pause, then, "Dylan is coming to think more and more of her too."

Jodie nodded, understanding where Bethan was headed, but not willing to discuss something like that. Not yet. She took a deep breath. "The air always smells sweeter out here."

"I suppose it does. The roses have lasted well this year too. It grew chilly early, but it hasn't grown any colder. Just day after day of the same beautiful Indian summer."

How strange it seemed, Jodie reflected to herself, that the evening was so natural, their talk so easy. As though it had only been four days since the last time they chatted. Not close on four years. Jodie realized that

Bethan's silence was an invitation for her to tell about her own life, but for some reason she continued to hold back. As though she wanted to take a while, grow accustomed to being here, in Harmony, with Bethan. And somehow Bethan seemed to understand, not pushing with even the smallest of questions, comfortable to just sit and rock and wait. Jodie glanced over at Bethan's calm, even features. She certainly had grown into a beautiful, serene young woman.

Heavy footsteps down the walk signaled another's approach. Then a cheerful voice said, "Well, would you just look at what we have here."

"Hello, Mr. Keane," Jodie said, recognizing the voice before the man came into view.

"Time's come for you to be calling me Gavin," he said, stepping forward with a broad grin and outstretched hands. He looked at her for a long time, seeming to size her up and liking what he found. "And I'll be calling you girl no longer."

She accepted his hug, then let him hold her at arm's length. The passage of time was clearly written upon his features. His hair had grayed, his eyes retreated a bit. His wife's illness had etched its way deeply into his being. For some reason, Jodie found the tears coming then, the ones which had not been there when she had been reunited with Bethan two hours earlier. Here in Gavin Keane's face was all the time lost, all the memories not shared, all the absence from friends so close she had come to think of them as family.

"My, but if you aren't a sight for sore eyes," Gavin said softly. Then he turned aside and said to the figure who had approached without Jodie realizing, "Ain't she turned into a beauty, Dylan?"

"She surely has," Dylan replied and stepped forward

into the light. "Hello, Jodie. How're you keeping?"

"Fine, Dylan." She had to stop and swallow hard. Even now the sight of him was unsettling—both for the memories and because even after all this time, despite all the sorrow which still weighed heavy upon him, he was such a handsome man. His smile was still there, just not as light as it had been, what with the shadow of pain still lingering. Somehow Jodie knew as soon as she took his hand, felt the strength and goodness course between them that he would soon be well again, deepened by the experiences but not broken. "Just fine."

Jodie's attention was pulled away from Dylan's face when Gavin spoke again. "Ain't this something," Bethan's father said, "my little girl all grown up and getting married. You met the groom yet?"

"Tomorrow," Bethan replied for her. "First thing."

"He's as fine a man as you'd ever care to meet," Gavin said, then clapped his son on the shoulder. "Come on, boy, let's leave these two to get on with their catching up."

He moved toward the kitchen door, turned, and called back over his shoulder, "Can't tell you how nice it is to have you back with us, Jodie, especially for such a time as this."

Dylan followed his father, but before he left he spoke in a soft voice for only Jodie's ears to hear. "Maybe you'd let me call on you?"

"I'd like that," she said as quietly as he.

Then he was gone, but Jodie felt her heart racing. What was he asking? What had she answered? Was she setting herself up for another deep and painful situation?

She pushed the thoughts from her mind and turned her attention back to Bethan. The night settled in closer around them on the swing, gracing them with an intimacy and peace that stretched out unbroken to the farthest horizon. Jodie sighed, feeling the calm work its way deep into her inner being. She reached down with a toe and gave a small push, assisting Bethan in keeping the swaying motion alive.

They stayed like that, silent and listening to the swing's gentle creak and the night's even softer sounds, until Jodie realized, "I haven't gotten a thing for you as a wedding present."

"Having you here to be my bridesmaid is the finest gift I could ever ask for," Bethan replied, her tone underscoring the truth of the statement.

"But I have to get you something," Jodie protested.

Bethan turned to her then, and it struck Jodie that her friend had been waiting for this moment, waiting ever since Jodie had called and said she was coming. Waiting and hoping. "There is only one gift I will accept from you, Jodie Harland," she said. "Would you pray with me?"

Jodie was surprised, yes. But not as much as she might have thought. Instead, there was a sense of epiphany to the moment. A sense of returning—but not to the past. Old tattered ends to woes and worries and unanswered questions weaved through her mind. And then the doubts and pressures settled and her mind stilled. With a strength of assurance so powerful, yet so gentle that it left no room for further question, Jodie knew this was the purpose of her coming home. She *knew* this.

She took a breath. The night had become utterly still, or perhaps she had momentarily lost the ability to hear or see beyond the porch and the moment and Bethan's request. Her mind settled further, as though the importance of this moment required her to focus as she had never done before, drawing not just her thoughts and her heart but her entire life down upon this instant. And this decision.

"All right," she whispered, and though the words were softly spoken and quickly released into the night, still their import left her shaking. It felt as though her entire being was resounding to a call of something unseen and unheard, yet so close that its power caused her to tremble from head to foot.

"Oh, thank you, thank you. You don't know what this means to me, how long I've dreamed of this moment." Bethan reached over and took her hand. "Shall I start?"

Jodie nodded and watched as Bethan lowered her head before bowing her own. The sense of presence enveloped her, so close she felt both surrounded and filled with its power. Gentle yet demanding. Urgently alive. Illuminating and joyous.

"Dear precious Father in heaven, you know my heart better than I know it myself," Bethan began, her voice full of emotion. You know I have prayed for this moment. You know how I love my sister Jodie, how I have missed her. How I have ached . . ."

Bethan had to stop there. Jodie listened to the sound of quiet weeping and felt the tears of her friend begin to dissolve any remaining barriers of her own heart. She released her hand from Bethan's, wiped her cheeks, then placed her arm around her friend's shoulders. The act seemed to give Bethan the strength to regain control. She reached over and took Jodie's other hand. Bethan managed a shaky breath, another, then continued, "I am happier than I have ever been in my entire life, Father. You have given me such a wonderful man, one who has asked me to be his bride, and now you have brought back to me my friend. I do not know anything else to say, Father, except thank you. Thank you for the blessings of this night. In Christ's holy name I pray, amen."

Jodie knew what needed to be said, knew the words were there waiting for her to speak. Yet still she waited a moment longer. There was no hurry. Not tonight.

"God, it has been so long since I have talked to you that I have forgotten how," Jodie said softly. "So I am going to have to let you speak for me."

Bethan started crying anew, and Jodie stopped for a moment and held her close, waiting with the patience of the love-filled night. When Bethan was quiet, Jodie continued, "I don't know what I have done to deserve a friend like this, but I thank you for her. I thank you for her prayers, and for her love, and for the fact that we are sitting here together again."

Jodie spent another long moment listening to the night and to her heart, gathering up all that needed to be said, before saying, "I thank you also for the power of your blessed forgiveness, which allows me to sit here and know that there is still a place in your family for me. I don't know how I know this, but I do. I am so sorry, Father, for turning away from you—from Bethan. I ask your forgiveness, and I thank you. In Jesus' name, amen."

"Amen," Bethan echoed, clasping Jodie's hand with both of hers. "Amen."

They stayed like that for a very long while, holding each other and listening to the night. And Jodie knew that here in this simple act of praying with her friend was the gift of finally returning home.

CHAPTER TWENTY-ONE

JODIE HUMMED AS SHE MOVED about the house. The housekeeper was not coming for the weekly cleaning, so Jodie tackled the job herself. She had never particularly enjoyed chores around the house, but today even scouring the stove and washing the floors could not dampen her spirits.

She wasn't sure where all this joy had come from, nor why it bubbled forth so exuberantly, lifting her spirits, making her feet light and her heart near to bursting. Her happiness seemed to brighten every dismal corner of the silent house. For that she was very thankful.

During the week since her arrival, Dylan had called on her several times. Though nothing had yet been said, Jodie knew in her heart that all she needed to do was give him a nod of encouragement. If she did, they could take up where they had so painfully left off four long years before.

Did she still love Dylan? She supposed there was something special about a first love. Something that was hard to let go.

But was that enough? Would there be days when she might wonder what could have been given to the world if she had kept her heart and mind fixed on her work in the lab?

As she dusted the front parlor, the thought came to her, an extension of the joy which filled her heart and mind to overflowing. She put down her cloth, straightened, and pondered the sudden mystery. She could pray for guidance. It seemed such a simple act, and yet so hard. It meant accepting the reality of what had been granted her ever since that evening on Bethan's porch. Not only that, it meant accepting the reality of its source.

She could pray for guidance. The wonder of those words filled her, melting away the barriers of pride and rejection. The answer would not come from her bright, reasoning mind, but rather from her awakening heart. God, the God she had rejected but to whom she had now returned, would show her what was right. Of that she felt confident.

So Jodie hummed.

------------ ✿ ------------

"I'm going to miss you, daughter."

Moira's words were almost gruff in her obvious attempt not to be maudlin. With a suddenness that surprised Bethan, she reached out swollen hands and pressed Bethan's head close to her breast.

"Oh, Momma," Bethan managed when she could trust her voice. "I feel so . . . so selfish. Being so happy when—"

Moira pushed her back so she could see her face and shook her shoulders gently. "Now is certainly not the time for nonsense, child. You don't even know how to be selfish. The good parson needs you just as bad as I do, and well we both know it."

Bethan nodded, the tears fresh on her cheeks. She did honestly feel that she could be a support for Connor in his work. The thought both pleased and frightened her. There was so much responsibility in being a pastor's wife. Bethan wiped her nose on her hankie and lifted her eyes to her mother. "Are you sure you'll be all right?"

"Maudie Herman is a fine woman. Fine. And strong as one of her husband's plowing horses," she said with an air of finality. "If she can't help me up and down the stairs and into my chair or bed on the bad days, nobody can, and that's the plain truth of it."

Bethan was still reluctant to desert her post and leave her mother in the care of another woman. She sniffed again.

"It won't be the same as having you here," Moira allowed. "But you can still stop by now and then, daughter. Pastor's not going to keep you home with ball and chain."

Bethan smiled and pushed back a wayward tress. "He says I ought to make a point of dropping in every single day."

"The man's generosity is touching," Moira said. "Tell him I'm grateful for his concern."

"Oh, Momma," Bethan said with the happiness shining from her eyes. "I can hardly believe the Lord has brought me such a good man."

Moira reached out and drew her daughter close once more, cradling the head against her shoulder, the swollen hands gently brushing back the strands of wisping hair. "Not one bit better than you be deserving," she said with deep feeling. "Not one bit."

CHAPTER TWENTY-TWO

EVERYONE AGREED IT WAS one of the finest weddings Harmony had ever known.

The bride was truly radiant. Her long dress somehow seemed whiter than white, seen as it was through the long flowing veil. And it was the veil that had everyone talking. Even before the ceremony began, the secret was out. The church was full of talk about how Moira had worked on the veil all summer long. She had apparently realized long before anyone else that this was coming, and she had known she would only be able to work on the veil a little at a time. When the wedding party finally made it up the aisle, Jodie bent over to gather the veil and send it flowing out in every direction, so all could admire Moira's handiwork. On a piece of almost transparent netting nine feet long, Moira had embroidered several *hundred* tiny pink rosebuds. Throughout the entire service, Jodie forced herself not to look in Moira's direction a single time. One glance at those swollen fingers knotted in Moira's lap, and Jodie knew she would not be able to stop herself from weeping.

After the service, the two ladies were driven over to Dylan's house to change, as Bethan's house was full of

213

preparations for the coming reception. It was a charming gingerbread house, with a broad roof sweeping down over a wraparound porch, and palest green shutters contrasting with the white wood. After she had helped Bethan out of her dress, Jodie went back downstairs. Kirsten was there to care for the children, and Jodie discovered she had grown into a wholesome, happy young woman, attractive in a fresh, country-girl fashion. There was now an aura of joy and peace along with a capable strength about her, enabling her to somehow be the same Kirsten grown older and someone else entirely, all at the same time.

Jodie asked about Kirsten's father since her mother's death, about Kirsten's work at the dry-goods store, and Jodie briefly mentioned her research work, to polite nods from Kirsten. They agreed that the wedding had been beautiful; Kirsten had stayed toward the back, watching over Dylan's children while their father stood up as Connor's best man. They then found themselves with nothing more to say.

After a silence that seemed uncomfortably long, Kirsten asked, "Would you like to see the children?"

"Oh yes."

Jodie followed Kirsten up the stairs and into the children's room. She was deeply moved by the sight of the beaming little girl who cooed and reached out both arms at Kirsten's entry. The crib had an arched canopy in fine ivory embroidery. With the smiling cherub dancing along the railing, the crib appeared to Jodie like a heavenly chariot, barely able to hold its beautiful passenger to the earth.

Kirsten cooed back, echoing the baby's sound. The child squealed with delight and danced upon chubby little legs, one hand curled around the slender white bannister, the other reaching tiny fingers toward Kirsten. The woman scooped up the child, nuzzled beneath the soft little chin, and the bright blue eyes in the little face almost closed with the happy pleasure. Small fists grabbed hold of Kirsten's brown curls as the child squealed with happiness.

Kirsten turned back toward Jodie in the doorway and said, both proud and shy, "This is Caroline."

Jodie smiled as the child turned about so she could watch Jodie from the safety of Kirsten's embrace. "She is a beautiful little girl," Jodie said. "How old is she?"

"Seven months," Kirsten said, nestling into the child's soft locks. "Her mother had a hard time with the birth. And then she got influenza. She passed on not long after. I suppose you've already heard all about that."

"Mama," the child announced softly, turning back to examine Kirsten's face.

Kirsten smiled. "The little one has been colicky and not eating well. But that's not much of a surprise, seeing how hard her start in this world was. All she needs is an extra helping of love."

There came a realization to Jodie then. One so filled with understanding that in its moment of arrival, Jodie knew that it was not herself thinking at all. Though such a revelation was illogical in her world, totally removed from her own scientific training, she *knew* this was not just a random thought. It was truly a gift. The thought was, *They belong together—this woman and child. I do not belong here, and this child is not mine to raise.*

With the acceptance of this truth, there came a sense of the entire room being filled with an invisible illumination. It was not a light for her eyes, but rather for her heart. She stood there in the doorway and felt the room become bathed in a light so strong and yet so gentle she could remain quiet and still, and watch as the deepest recesses of her own heart were revealed. It united them all, the child and this young woman and herself, bonded together with a love so pure and so overwhelming that there was suddenly no longer room for doubt or questioning. None at all. She had her answer.

CHAPTER TWENTY-THREE

JODIE PAUSED AT THE CORNER where Bethan's lovely little cottage came into view and tucked a lace-trimmed hankie back into her pocket. She had cried for quite long enough. There would be no more tears. She was surprised that she had allowed them at all this morning. She had thought that she had done all her weeping the night before.

It had not been an easy evening. The time of letting go had surrounded her with surprising force. She had found herself totally unprepared for all the deep emotions that had filled her, as the pillow had soaked up her tears and God had erased her bitterness. She had been carrying such a load of pain, guilt, and anger. All the burdens had come pouring out—at Bethan for taking Dylan, at God for taking her mother, at her father for locking himself away from her and retreating into his own silent, lonely world.

But as the night had worn on, God had helped her to work through the pain. Now she understood that much of it had been of her own making. She could have reached out for comfort and healing. There were those who would have gladly given it, especially her Lord. She

JANETTE OKE & T. DAVIS BUNN

should have realized, should have understood. And the force of what she had caused herself to lose had made the night longest of all.

Toward dawn, when sorrow had finally given way to quiet reflection, she began to realize that though it was not an easy victory she now faced, yet she had gained so very much. She was now free to embrace life in a totally new fashion. Free to forgive and reach out to her father. Free to accept and return Bethan's friendship in full measure. Even free to wish Dylan and his little family— and Kirsten—God's full blessing. It was truly a new and beautiful beginning, one full of promise and adventure.

She had been locked in a self-imposed shell, stiff and serious and afraid to feel. But that was in the past now. She was free, in many senses for the very first time, liberated to live and laugh—and love.

Jodie started forward, her sadness over leaving again now behind her. In its place was a smile of new beginnings, and anticipation over what was to come, and what awaited her in Raleigh.

Lowell would be so surprised at the changes in her, she reflected, and the thought brought a new bounce to her stride. She tried to push it away as she approached Bethan's front porch, but the thought of Lowell was not that easily vanquished. Working together suddenly seemed like a good idea. So good that she felt an eagerness to share her feelings with him and get started. Perhaps she should stop off on the way to the station and send him a wire, she mused, surprising even herself with the unfamiliar thought.

She smiled again as she spotted Bethan sitting comfortably within the porch's shade. Somewhere deep inside a feeling of warmth spread through her whole being. It was time to leave, yes, but without the sad endings of her earlier departure. This time, she was only making room for new beginnings.

Their honeymoon had been two weeks of bliss down on the Carolina coast. Even so, Bethan had been positively delighted to return. Now that she was settling into her home, Bethan could scarcely imagine life without Connor.

With a gift from her parents and another from the church, they had managed to take up residence in a little cottage just a stone's throw from where she had been raised. It even had a small front porch and a swing. Which was where she was when Jodie arrived, a half-filled pan of freshly shelled peas in her lap.

Jodie stopped and surveyed the homey scene, then laughed out loud. "If you don't look like a happily married woman, I don't know who does."

"It's been an easy adjustment—and wonderful," Bethan agreed merrily, wiping her brow with the edge of her apron. Damp tendrils wisped about her cheeks. "Look at me. Sitting here wiping my brow. Whoever would have thought we'd have such fine weather right on into November."

Bethan rose to her feet, picked up the pan, and started for the door. "Come on inside. I've got a fresh pitcher of lemonade, and there's bread about ready to come out of the oven. Connor promised to stop by around this time." She turned and smiled down at where Jodie stood. "If you've got time, you could run an errand with me this afternoon. I promised Old Mr. Russel I'd stop by. I'll bet his dog Sherman still remembers you."

"I can't stay," Jodie said quietly.

Something in her tone caused Bethan to turn back around. A funny fear coursed through her. "Why, what's the matter?"

"Nothing's wrong," Jodie replied.

Bethan studied her friend's face. She did not look troubled or anxious. In fact, there was a tranquillity in her eyes that Bethan had not seen before.

"I was just wondering if you'd walk me down to the station. I'm catching the five o'clock train," Jodie continued.

Bethan set the pot down before she dropped it. "Back to Raleigh? Now?"

"I've got some decisions I can't put off any longer. About work and what I'm going to be doing next. I've already been gone far too long." The words spilled out, tumbling over one another in the hurried effort to be said and done. "I have work waiting, Bethan. It's important to me, and it's what I do best."

Bethan had to struggle to find the words. "But I thought, I hoped—"

Jodie did not allow her to continue. "It wouldn't work," she said. "It's not right."

"Not right? I'm sure he still loves you, Jodie. At least, he could come to love you again. I can see it in his eyes, hear it in his voice."

Jodie's gaze was steady. "And what about Kirsten?"

"Kirsten—I think she'd—get over it," Bethan said, almost desperate. "And Dylan would—"

Jodie stepped forward and placed her hands on Bethan's gingham-clad arms. "Listen to me," she said, her voice urgent. "Kirsten loves him. She *loves* him. The children too. And they love her. You've seen her with them. She's the one who has been there, cared for them, brought order and security back to their lives. She loves them like they were her own."

Bethan blinked back tears. "I know," she whispered.

"I can't do it," Jodie said. "I could never break another woman's heart like . . ."

"Oh, Jodie." Bethan hugged her close. "You don't know how sorry—I never meant . . ."

"I'm sorry too," Jodie interrupted. "But not for the reason you are thinking. You were right. It would have been all wrong," she said, then paused before continuing, "It's taken me a long time, too long, to learn what forgiveness really means."

They held each other for the longest time, neither willing to let go, as though both were storing up a closeness deprived them for far too long. Finally Jodie whispered, "We need to be going."

Bethan nodded, wiped her eyes, and took a long breath. "Where are your things?"

"This is all I'm taking. I'm leaving my case here. I plan to be back more often nowadays." She smiled as she walked down the path to the main road. "I've been thinking about maybe buying myself a car."

"A car!" Bethan was glad for a reason to laugh. "Jodie Harland, what on earth will you think of next?"

"Daddy needs me to keep reminding him there's a world out there." Jodie hesitated, then went on, "And after these past few weeks of thinking and praying, I feel like maybe I might have found the answer he's been needing to hear."

Bethan reached over, took her best friend's hand. "I'll be praying for you."

Jodie nodded. "I know now how much I need it. I'll never deny that again." She hesitated, then added quietly, "I already see a lot of places where I need to put faith to work. And there's someone who has long needed to hear me practice the lesson of forgiveness."

Bethan started to ask her what she meant, but something in Jodie's faraway gaze held her back. They walked on in silence for a time, until Bethan said quietly, "I don't know who this mysterious someone is." She stopped and stole a sideways glance at Jodie. "I have the feeling that you are going to go out there and accomplish great things."

Jodie pushed open the train window, pulled out her lace-edged linen handkerchief, and whisked the tears from her cheeks with one quick motion, as though defying them to dampen her skin again. She leaned forward and looked down to where Bethan stood and managed a smile. "Don't you dare let me go," Jodie said. "Not from your heart. Not from where it matters. If you don't hold on, I'll fly off with no past and no direction."

"Not ever again," Bethan promised. "What will you be doing?"

"I'm not certain. The university and two companies are all pressing me for an answer. Politely, but pressing just the same." Again there was a new sense of hesitation, a moment of reaching beyond herself, as though it was finally all right not to have all the answers. "I feel like maybe it's a decision I need to make only after some more prayer."

"You don't know," Bethan told her, "how wonderful it is to hear you say those words."

The whistle blew a single long blast. Jodie reached down with both hands and grabbed hold of Bethan's upstretched fingers. "You have to promise to let me be the second person to know whenever a little Connor or another sweet Bethan is on the way."

"I promise, I promise," Bethan said, walking down the tracks as the train started chuffing away, still holding to Jodie's outstretched hands. "But it won't be a Bethan."

A final squeeze, and Jodie felt the train's speed pull her hands free. "I love you!"

"I've already talked to Connor," Bethan called. "If God ever blesses us with a girl, we're going to name her Jodie, after my very best friend."

The train moved on, picking up speed, sending out great gusts of billowing smoke. Bethan pulled out the hankie and waved it over her head. Jodie leaned from the window of the moving passenger car watching the young woman and the town of Harmony grow smaller. Her eyes misted, but there was comfort in knowing that she'd be back. Soon. She'd be back.

Bethan stood and waved as the forests and the sunlight and the distance swallowed up the train and her friend. She kept waving for a long time afterward, even though her eyes were dimmed by tears, and all she could make out was a shining golden haze.